"Tabbie's original and unusual plots and storylines make for a really intriguing read."
        Dave Andrews, Presenter, *BBC Radio Leicester*

"The master of supernatural suspense."
        Peter J Bennett, *Author*

"The books are catching, they keep you thinking, and make you 'look outside the box'. I enjoy reading Tabbie's books in my limited down time."
        Anne Royle and Spook (my four legged glasses).
        Founder *Pathfinder Guide Dog Programme*

To Shona
Best Wishes
Tabbie

The Paws Of Spiritual Justice

Other Books by this Author

THE JENNY TRILOGY
White Noise is Heavenly Blue
The Spiral
Choler

A Fair Collection
The Unforgiveable Error
No-Don't!
Above The Call
A Bit Of Fresh
A Bit Of Spare

Visit the author's website at:
www.tabbiebrowneauthor.com

The Paws Of Spiritual Justice

Tabbie Browne

Copyright © 2017 Tabbie Browne

All rights reserved, including the right to reproduce this book, or portions thereof in any form. No part of this text may be reproduced, transmitted, downloaded, decompiled, reverse engineered, or stored, in any form or introduced into any information storage and retrieval system, in any form or by any means, whether electronic or mechanical without the express written permission of the author.

This is a work of fiction. Names and characters are the product of the author's imagination and any resemblance to actual persons, living or dead, is entirely coincidental.

The views expressed in this work are solely those of the author and do not necessarily reflect the views of the publisher, and the publisher hereby disclaims any responsibility for them.

ISBN: 978-0-244-34006-3

PublishNation
www.publishnation.co.uk

THIS BOOK IS DEDICATED TO

A N N

Now in spirit

The loving mother of Sarah
and Lou
(whose eyes are watching you from the front cover)

*She was the most kind,
caring and selfless
Mum you ever could
have wished for
Lou*

*She was someone we
always looked up to
and could talk to about
anything. She was an amazing Mum
Sarah*

Please note Ann and her daughters bear no resemblance whatever to the characters in this story, in fact just the opposite.

The author wishes to extend her grateful thanks to Lou for kindly granting permission for her image to be used

IN MEMORY OF
C O N K E R
2004 – 2017

This beautiful all white short haired cat
was my constant companion in my office.
Quite a character but could be a bit of a naughty boy.

He took over my 'in box'
and it was his permanent spot while I was at my desk.
When he wanted my attention, usually for food, he would walk
across in front of the monitor and stand there.

Being upstairs it was also a perfect vantage point
for him to chatter to the birds on the opposite roof.

His image will live on as it appears on the cover of CHOLER
and, as was his usual practice when being photographed,
he was in full yawn.

It seems poignant that he should pass over
right in the middle of this novel about cats in spirit.

But he and Kath have pushed me to get it finished
and you don't argue do you?

Chapter 1

"Now what are you looking at?"

June took off her glasses and her eyes went in the direction of the cat's stare. She looked back at him.

"There's nothing there Wiz. Now stop it."

The name was short for Wizard which he had been given as a kitten when his long black fur looked almost like a little cloak, and his yellow eyes looked right into your soul.

The sound of the doorbell made June give a short laugh.

"Ah, you knew someone was coming. Bet it's Daph."

As she greeted her sister at the front door she said that Wiz must have known she was there.

"Hmm. Never liked it. Gives me the creeps."

Daphne came into the room and plonked her bags on the nearest chair.

"Hope there's no cat hairs on there." She muttered.

"No more than usual." Was the short reply.

Although June was always pleased to see her sibling, it rankled that there were always snide remarks about Wiz and the reference to him as 'it'. Having been widowed for some time, she was grateful for the constant companionship, but the cat made it obvious he wasn't pleased when 'intruders' came into his space. Daphne on the other hand was married and was not a cat or dog person which was why she probably didn't mind offending people with her comments.

After the usual small talk the ladies sat down with a coffee and Daph soon started bragging about where they were thinking of going on holiday. The conversations rarely varied from what she and her husband were doing, and she never asked how her sister was coping.

Wizard turned away from them, not from boredom, but because he was picking up something in his vicinity. Even with his extra sensory vision he couldn't see anything but he knew something was taking temporary refuge in his space. If Daphne had only known what may be taking place inches from her coffee cup she would have been out of the house in a flash for not only did she not like pets, she was terrified of anything 'unnatural' as she called it.

The air was slowly getting colder. The cat's back was rising in anticipation for he knew something was near. While he, like most animals are thought to be able to see things people can't, he was very territorial and hated anything in his area, so passing through or not, he wanted them gone. He was conscious of a shape forming just above Daphne's head. For a moment it hovered then seemed to grow until it was standing behind her. Still Wizard watched.

"Have you got any heating on? I'm frozen." Daphne visibly shuddered and rubbed her arms.

"Of course I have." June was always annoyed at the way her sister snapped instead of asking a question in a civilised manner.

"Doesn't feel like it. You trying to save money or something?"

"No. The central heating is on."

Although she tried to sound matter of fact, June had to admit to herself that the room had suddenly dropped in temperature. To keep the peace she added "I'll turn it up a bit."

As she stood at the control in the hall, the door to the lounge closed slowly. When she turned round she thought it strange but assumed she had shut it without realising, but why would she do that? Grabbing the handle she tried to open it but it wouldn't move. Then she heard the most frightening scream coming from the room and just as she was desperately struggling with the handle, the door burst open almost sending her flying in.

"What on earth's the matter with you?" She yelled.

The sight that met her was unbelievable. Daphne was on the floor clutching at her throat, her clothing in disarray and a look of terror on her face.

"Get me out of here. I've been attacked." The words stumbled out.

"Don't be silly, I've only been gone seconds." June, although not liking what she was seeing was more annoyed than anything.

"What do you mean?" Daphne tried to get up. "Look at me. It attacked me."

June had to admit something had happened but in such a short time it didn't seem possible. So had her sister done this to herself for some reason?

"It's that animal. You should get rid of it." Daphne was stabbing at the air as if trying to point at Wizard.

"What animal, as you call it?" June was seething now.

"That….that…. where is it?"

"If you mean Wiz, he's left and I'm not surprised. You've frightened him."

It took a few moments for the atmosphere to calm down, but after the ladies had regained their composure and their seats, June said she wanted to know exactly what had happened when she left the room. Daphne was rather reluctant at first because anything bordering on something that couldn't be explained sent her almost into shock. As nothing seemed to be forthcoming, June went to check on Wiz's whereabouts and found him sitting on a stool in the kitchen and decided that while she was there she would make some more coffee.

"Here you are, you look as though you could do with it." She said pushing the cup towards her sister. "Now, are you going to tell me or leave me guessing?"

She sat in the chair where she could face her and waited.

"Well, I was cold."

There was a long pause and June remained silent waiting for the other one to continue.

"Then when you went out I felt something holding me."

"Go on. What kind of... something?" The last word was emphasised.

"I don't know. I don't know. It was big, like a person and it got me from behind and pulled me down."

June hid a smile. "And you are saying it was Wiz?"

"Well. No. I mean at first I thought it must be but......" her voice trailed off.

"Did you see anything? Anything at all?" June was pushing.

"Not actually see."

"So you didn't. You didn't see Wiz, You didn't see a person. In fact you imagined it all."

Daphne was fuming now. "No I did not imagine it. Something attacked me."

"Oh not again. We're going round in circles." June eyed her up and down. "You're not on those pills again are you, only they did send you rather strange last time?"

"I get it. You're trying to say I'm losing my mind. Well I know what happened here and I'll tell you something for nothing. I won't be setting foot in here again. If you can't see it you must be blind or you are behind it."

"What?" June was staggered but then a thought hit her. What is she going to say to Ken when she get's home? He's going to be asking questions and always takes his wife's side. Keeping her composure she stood up.

4

"I think that is a very good idea Daph. Go home and sort your brain out. There is nothing going on here apart from me living my quiet little life disturbing nobody."

At which point she noticed her gathering up her coat, had a quick look at her neck as she was helping her on with it and was certain it had all been a little ruse to get her attention or sympathy for something but whatever her game, it hadn't worked. She closed the door behind her and was relieved to have the place to herself again.

"Oh you've come back in." She jumped as she saw Wiz had returned to his favourite spot on the edge of the table and was eying her quizzically, his tail slowly waving to and fro. Was that a smirk on his face?

"No." She thought. "Impossible."

Although it is an accepted fact that there are helpers in the spirit world as well as in earthly form, not so much is heard of helper animals. Fortunately it has become common place to see a guide or hearing dog and those who assist the disabled in so many ways. The list of working dogs is endless from military, police and customs to some unsavoury tasks such as cadaver searching. But that is only a part of their existence. Whether in body or spirit, they work just as hard using the skills learned on earth to help many other forms of existence. Some are so highly adept, they can complete their task and leave before they have even been traced if they so wish. But there are also times when their presence can have a profound effect and the perpetrators wish they hadn't encountered them. The dogs leave with the thought "They won't do that again in a hurry!"

But what about cats? Owners will tell you they know when one of their departed companions is around. Some even feel them on the bed, but can see nothing, but simply being in presence isn't being a helper. Well, be prepared for a shock, for you are about to embark into a world you couldn't possibly imagine. You will travel to other dimensions, your mind will let you experience feelings you could never possibly dream about and you will never look at anything the same again. If you think this is too much to handle, now is the time to stop. Go no further. But if you do, you will not be reading a story, you will be sharing an experience.

One of the most unnerving things cats do is to look to the side of you or even appear to be looking at something behind you. They will even move their heads sideways to get a better view. But we see nothing. As long as we are not aware of any hostile feelings, we tend to get on with whatever we were doing and pass it of as 'the cat's freaking out again.' However, if there is a sudden chill and the hairs on your back react, there is something not too good in presence. Sometimes you experience a warm glow and the love of a past relative or pet, or even a smell which relates to the individual, but that is a totally different experience.

As with human existence in its various forms, cats exist on many levels and no one knows just how far up the ladder they go, but there are theories that they exceed anything the most learned and experience forms have ever reached.

The likes of Wizard just tick along on the lower planes noticing passing traffic but rarely getting involved but often they are the ones who are used to watch unobtrusively. When the visitor approached Daphne, he recognised him immediately. In fact the entire spirit world was aware of him. This man had led an evil life attacking middle aged women and had met an untimely end at the hands of one of the husbands. But it didn't finish there. Like a soul in torment he travelled the lower spiritual levels finding as many victims as he could, attempting to kill them too. To start with it was nothing more than a strange feeling. Women would shudder and say it was as though something was crawling over them, but now his power was growing, hence the evidence left on Daphne. Sentinels had been allotted to move him to another zone, but were limited as he could only travel on low levels. They had intervened at June's house and only left when they were sure it was safe.

As the danger had passed and there was no chance of him returning, the watch on June went back to normal. But one person had also arrived, her late husband. He looked as his wife with such love and affection gently slipping his arm around her. She stopped, smiled and put her hand to her shoulder gently sniffing the air. It was there, the smell of tomatoes growing on the plants he kept in the greenhouse and she didn't feel alone. This was one person Wizard allowed into his space and although he hadn't known him in body, he instinctively knew who he was. He watched them for a moment then curled up with his back to them, one paw across his face.

If June's house normally had an air of peace about it, a few miles away in another village things were very different. With earthly beings, groups are formed for people with the same interest, and the same occurs in the spiritual field but often for more sinister intents. Although there is a continual fight between good and bad, there are many different kinds of evil and it takes specialists in each field to combat and destroy these elements. Rather the same as you wouldn't send an orthopaedic surgeon to do brain surgery, each has their own talent.

In general terms there are many militant sectors tackling the ongoing battles but on different levels. The likes of Daphne's molester was small fry but the guardians of the peace never dismissed such assaults, as they could be hiding much greater powers who were simply using the underlings to gain knowledge or scan the area, plus any active cell wouldn't want June to get wind of them.

This lady was in tune spiritually in a mild way but that wasn't to say she wouldn't be suspicious if the vibes didn't feel right. It was decided that extra watch should be put on her from a distance, just to be safe.

The active cell was about ten miles away, but it wasn't stationary. In order not to be tracked, it was continually on the move but still keeping within the area. Mainly it consisted, as many did, of little upstarts who thought themselves much better than anyone else but didn't have the ability to act alone so they joined up but that was a problem. The ones who wanted to take charge were always fighting amongst themselves as to who was the boss. To the good forces these groups were more of an annoyance than a threat although they could always be groomed by higher more powerful sects.

A cat watcher from a higher source had been in observing from a distance when Daphne was attacked and was quick to pick up her dislike of animals, also a rather sadistic streak in her temperament. Although it was a chance encounter, he knew this woman could be used as a tool against them by any opposing evil foe. He waited until the juvenile cell had finished their bit of fun then repositioned himself at Daphne's home.

"Well I shan't be going back there in a hurry I can tell you." She ranted at her husband when he came home from work.

"Going where?"

Ken was trying to get his coat off and have a cup of tea without his wife bending his ear.

"To our June's of course. Where do you think I mean?"

He sighed.

"Why?"

"Why? Why do you think? I've told you before, there's things going on in that house and it's not natural." She gave a huff as if it backed up her words.

He looked round for his slippers.

"I'm not with you." Was all he could think of to say. If she'd got a bee in her bonnet, why on earth not just come out with it. All this talking in riddles went over him.

"She's up to something, and that cat's got a lot to do with it."

Still at a loss Ken almost laughed.

"You'll be saying she's into witchcraft next."

"Don't even joke about it." Her fist came down on the table.

"Steady on." He looked serious now. "You can't go accusing your own sister of things like that."

"Well you mark my words. We'll see." Her attitude was one of satisfaction.

They were quiet while she made some tea, and as he drank he paused and said very quietly "And what would you do if your suspicions held water?"

"What? Well, I mean I haven't got any proof. Yet." She added quickly.

"You telling me you'd shop her?"

Daphne was getting very flustered now.

"Well we couldn't ignore it could we?"

"Now just a moment, what's all this 'we' business?" He put his cup down. "Don't include me, and if you take my advice you'll keep your nose out as well."

"Oh I see." She looked really put out now. "It can go on but we must turn a blind eye."

He sighed heavily and tried to change the subject.

"Are we going down the Swan for a drink tonight?"

"Might as well." She shrugged.

"If we do," he paused to make sure she was listening "for heavens sake don't go sounding off about what you've been saying. Keep it quiet. At least for now."

She sniffed by way of answer.

"I mean it." He emphasised. "That's not for other ears. And you haven't any proof."

"I suppose." She said begrudgingly, but thought "I can just tell Mary, she won't breathe a word."

The evil cell was plotting its next annoying attack. It wouldn't return to June's and having had a good laugh at Daphne, had exhausted its fun there. But where next?

If they thought they were alone, it showed just how naïve they were for every group, and even those working alone were being constantly monitored by higher levels always ready to intervene when needed to keep innocent souls safe. Most of the protectors, as they were called were known. Some even were referred to by a name or tag so that they could be identified. But there were also those who operated well under cover, were seldom seen but you knew when they had been and sorted something. It was also suspected that some of the highly skilled spirits were seen and were working in full view, but in fact reverted to their true selves when needed.

However, way above any of these, were The Paws. Their entire existence was unknown on any level. They would watch and plan but when they moved in, absolutely no power could detect them. They were not seen, heard or their presence felt. Such was their skill, they could move without even disturbing the surrounding air or leaving a wake which was unheard of. When they took on a task, there were rumours in the spirit world that something had been at work, but not a soul knew who or what.

Chapter 2

The Swan was quite busy as it was quiz night in the lounge and the bar had its usual regulars debating the topics of the day. Daphne had made sure Mary would be there so that she could offload her latest tale while Ken had his usual game of darts with some of his mates.

"Who are you looking for? Your eyes have been fixed on that door since we sat down?"

Ken couldn't help but notice where his wife's attention had been.

"Oh just wondered who'd be in tonight for me to talk to while you're playing." She tried to sound offhand but he wasn't convinced. He knew her too well and most of his time was spent wondering what gossip she was receiving and passing on.

"Just remember what I said." He picked up his beer.

"Don't be so silly. You do over react sometimes." Her manner was meant to put him in his place but she secretly wished he wouldn't pay so much attention to her every move.

"Hello you two."

The interruption was well timed as Mary arrived as if on cue, and sat beside Daphne. Ken, as usual, offered to get her a drink and made his way to the bar before she could go into her usual spiel of how kind he was and surely it must be her turn to pay. If she had a purse, he'd never seen it.

"Mary. Do me a favour. When we are talking, don't look too interested."

Daphne knew she would be scrutinised and wanted to appear as though they were just exchanging women's talk.

"Why? What's going on?" Mary's eyes lit up.

"That's what I mean. He'll know."

"He'll know what?"

Nice as she was, Mary wasn't always very quick on the uptake and wanted everything explained in triplicate before she got the message.

"Just wait until he's playing." Daphne almost hissed in her ear.

"Ooo. Sounds exciting."

"Shh. He's coming."

"There you are Mary, make it last. Going to be busy tonight and could take a long time to get served." Ken was trying to hide his sarcasm but it was lost on the women who couldn't wait to start chatting.

As he sat down he ventured "Why don't you two give the quiz a go? Make a nice change."

"We're alright here." Daphne retorted, after all how could she tell Mary things while they were in a quiz?

Mary nodded in agreement, so that idea went down like a fart in church.

To say the air was a little tense until the match started was putting it mildly, but once it was under way Daphne nudged her friend. She was glad of the noise as it would drown the conversation but that proved to be a bit of a disadvantage when Mary couldn't quite make out what she was saying and she ended up almost mouthing it to her.

"And there I was, on the floor with this thing attacking me."

Mary still wasn't quite getting the gist of it.

"But you haven't told me what it looked like."

"Christ Almighty. I couldn't see it."

"Right." Mary's face was blank.

"Pay attention. I was in June's lounge. Something or someone got me by the throat, on the ground, and was biting me and hitting me and trying to force its way onto me."

"Oh so June did it!" Mary's eyes were wide open now and if the room had been quiet the remark would have been heard by the entire assembly.

"No. For God's sake. No." Daphne was reaching exasperation level.

"Oh. I get it."

"Thank goodness for small mercies." But relief was short lived.

"You mean the cat attacked you. Oh I thought it was going to be something more juicy than that." Disappointment was all over her face.

Daphne took a deep breath.

"No Mary. The cat did not attack me. June did not attack me. So what does that leave?" Her eyes went up waiting for the answer.

There was a short pause but the reply was beyond belief.

"Oh, either you imagined it or……I know, you're having me on aren't you?"

This time the pause was a long one while Daphne was trying to decide whether it was worth continuing with this. Normally, Mary was an eager listener, didn't contribute much and loved secrets which was why she could be trusted with anything. So much so that she wouldn't even repeat it to the person who told her! She didn't have many friends as most people found her hard work. Still unmarried, she lived in hope of finding her Mr Right one day and she was certain that he would come along and it would all be romantic and beautiful.

Ken came and sat down waiting for his next turn and asked casually what the two girls had been gossiping about.

"Oh nothing much." Daphne was quick to reply. "Can't hear yourself think,"

He nodded almost relieved but he knew his wife only too well and was sure that wasn't the end of it.

As soon as he left again Mary asked "So I got it right didn't I?"

By way of reply Daphne looked her straight in the eye and shook her head.

"Oh so you were serious."

"Yes Mary I was deadly serious."

"So, what was it? I don't quite get that bit."

"Spiritual my dear girl."

Mary thought for a moment then utter shock came over her face.

"No! But that's impossible"

"Afraid not. It was as real as if you had got hold of my arm like this."

To emphasize the point, she grabbed Mary's wrist in a vice like grip.

"That hurts."

"Exactly." Daphne made sure Ken was playing then pulled her top down to expose the bruises on her neck.

"Oh. He did that to you?" Mary looked straight toward Ken.

"No. Not him. It."

"But a ghost couldn't do that. It's impossible."

"Well here's the evidence." Daphne covered her neck.

Mary was obviously deep in thought and came out with possibly the most sensible thing she had said all night.

"Don't you think you should show the vicar? They know about this sort of thing, that's what they are there for."

This put Daphne in an awkward spot. She didn't go to church and didn't feel you could only ask for help just when you needed it. Also, there was something in her inner self that made her uncomfortable about religion. She had never like being forced to go when she was little and felt they were all a load of hypocrites. In fact she felt out of place in any church and only went for weddings and funerals. The two sat in silence for a while both mulling over the facts.

But if they thought they were not being observed they were very wrong. The spirit that had attacked Daphne had drawn the attention of its group to believe that this contact could be developed further. Here was a target that would lean towards evil rather than good given the right encouragement, and if they caught plenty of her kind early enough, they could all be groomed to carry out whatever evil tasks they were given. Therefore, if they steered Daphne towards consulting the vicar, they could also gain a foothold in the church, and then they could really go to work.

Their attention also turned to Mary. Just the opposite to her friend. Never married, went to church regularly, always said her prayers, only thought good of people, in fact just too pure. But instead of disregarding her, what a conquest she would be if she too could be dragged into the fold. So Daphne had unwittingly exposed her to a fate worse than anyone could imagine, possible eternal possession.

"It's the beer leg." Ken announced as he broke into their thoughts.

"What already?" Daphne had been so engrossed trying to get the facts through to Mary, she hadn't noticed the time. When he left the table to return to the game, the two looked at each other.

"Well, are you going to?" Mary wanted to know. "Because I'm sure the one at our church would speak to you."

"What are you on about?" Daphne turned a bit sharply.

"Seeing a vicar."

"Oh, I'm not sure. Anyway I don't think it will happen again."

Mary wasn't giving up. "But if it does, then will you think about it?"

"Alright, alright, I promise I will give it some thought."

As far as the ladies were concerned that seemed to end the matter for now, but in the unseen realms plans were underway to get these two groomed into the ways of a very unsavoury existence.

But while the evil plotters were concentrating on their objective, they too were under scrutiny by the protective angels who were determined that in this case they would never succeed.

And although the good powers were aware that the cat patrols were also taking note, they left them to their own devices as long as they didn't hinder them. It was only on certain occasions that different spiritual beings worked together.

The Paws, possessing ultimate skills and of such an extremely high level, always worked alone, although they milked others for information. They never interacted at close range with any other source but monitored everything. If they issued an order it was assumed it had come from another power. They had an uncanny instinct to sense when they should take an interest in a particular situation and at which point to become actively involved. Unbeknown to the likes of Wizard, they had him upload any aspect that could spell danger, and when June's house had been visited, his observations had been noted and spiritually logged. They could hack into anything without exception. If knowledge existed in any form, they would be aware of it. There was no other group or power to equal them, yet without proof of their existence, they were only a myth.

They had been spread around the globe on various tasks of late, each cat being so skilled they only joined forces when extreme measures were called for.

As with all spirits they needed no name or particular sex, but often chose to adopt one purely by choice.

The most senior was known as Marmaduke and when difficult decisions had to be made often had the last word.

There is always a character in any group and Bracket was no exception, but for all his nonchalant ways, he was very highly tuned and sensed everything just before it happened.

The serious one was always changing his moniker and had recently moved from Hamish to Hashtag, because he liked the sound of it. But he was up to date on anything to do with technology and sometimes was waiting for the humans to catch up with him.

Those currently using the female form were -

Bonnet, who regardless of gender was always the sweetest nature and gave the impression no-one could upset her, but that was her disguise, for underneath she was like steel, solid and unbending.

Ampersand let you think that she never took any notice and nothing mattered, but every minute detail was stored in her knowledge like a never ending encyclopaedia.

Sunset could only be described as the quiet one. But you know what they say about still waters.

So this skilful band, whether working alone or as one had taken on some of the most dangerous and deadly forces known, and probably some unknown. But that information would never be divulged.

Something about the recent increase of disturbed air around the villages had alerted Bracket's senses and he immediately sent the feeling to the rest of the group. They had all encountered such a thing many times before and knew that it may be nothing but often resulted in the start of something disastrous. Plagues and wars had often had small beginnings which had turned into world wide events and in the current era of biological warfare the threat could mean global death.

The first task was to identify the cause of the disturbance for they didn't just happen, someone or something always had to start it going and then it grew as it goaded others into its grasp.

Bracket didn't have to be anywhere near the place to get his information. The group were like orbiting satellites, always observing from afar but knew every detail. They only made close contact when the situation demanded it.

He was combing the villages sensing a few little incidents similar to Daphne's experience, always a sole offender but not the same one. This told him there had to be a sect working together and it wouldn't be just for their sadistic pleasure, although that would probably feature in their operation.

His attention homed in to the two ladies who were now getting ready to go home from The Swan.

"We'll drop you off, won't we Ken?" Daphne nudged his arm.

"Course we will. Can't have you walking the streets on your own." He laughed at Mary.

She tried to look coy but it went unnoticed.

It was only a short drive and the pair waited for her to get indoors and put the light on before they drove off. She gave a little wave and closed the door.

"Pity she never found a bloke." Ken said as he pulled away.

"Well, I've tried to get her to brighten herself up a bit. I mean she did get friendly with that one lad but then he went off and married that slut from the house near the grange."

"But that was years ago. It's like she's not bothered." He was insistent.

"Well it's her choice." Daphne considered the matter closed.

"Waste of a good woman if you ask me." He grinned.

"Well I don't ask you and you can stop being coarse, I know what you men have in your minds."

"And what's wrong with that?" He almost shouted. "It's natural, and you never refused I notice."

"But we're married. It's different."

They travelled in silence as her thoughts turned back to the attack earlier. She had examined herself when she got home and there were no marks on her so was it possible she had imagined it?

"No." She told herself. It had all been too real but who would believe her? June hadn't and she had witnessed the door being closed so she must know something, and so Daphne decided that whatever it was, she was going to find out before it happened again.

Mary closed the door, the noise of the pub still ringing in her ears. She knew she had to settle before she could go to bed so decided to make a cup of hot chocolate. As she stood in the small kitchen she felt something encompassing her from behind but as she tried to turn it held her firmly against the working surface. Fearing an intruder, she started to tremble but tried to reach for something as a defence. Then she realised that although she could feel the force holding her body, when she looked down there was nothing visible. Again she struggled but the hold got tighter until she could hardly breathe. There was now something feeling its way up her legs until it reached her groin. A faint cry came out of her mouth and suddenly she was released. She stood there alone looking round the kitchen but everything was untouched and exactly the same as it was. The chocolate in the mug a few inches from her was motionless so nothing had disturbed it in the slightest. She picked it up and went into the lounge and sat in the arm chair. All Daphne's words now seemed to make sense.

"It happened to her!" At last it seemed to have got through to her. "And now it's happened to me." Her mouth dropped open as she realised that her friend hadn't been fabricating the whole thing. She felt a little guilty at having dismissed it, but she would explain at the first opportunity that now she understood. At least she thought she did.

Bracket was aware that the activity was being monitored on lower levels for which he was grateful in some ways for it gave protection to the targeted victims, but sometimes it could hamper their plans especially if it was only the tip of a much larger operation.

It was time to set on deputies. He selected several cats living in the area which he knew were fairly high on the spiritual level and set them to observe everything that appeared foreign in any way. They didn't have to do anything by way of reporting as he could pick up their thoughts. It was no good having any that were easily distracted, so he was very careful in his choice. Also they had to realise that they didn't question their orders and they had no idea who was dishing them out. It has to be remembered that this was still all being controlled from a great distance, and Bracket would not communicate with lower levels unless in an emergency. Therefore none of the observers had any idea who was controlling them but these had been used before and knew the drill.

Ken unlocked the front door and as Daphne followed him in she stumbled.

"What's up?" He turned as she nearly knocked him over.

"Feel strange." Her colour had drained and he thought she was going to pass out.

"Stay where you are." He said. "Don't try to get up for a minute."

She was mumbling about something on her back, then on her legs and her hands were going all over her body as though she was trying to ward something off.

Her early rant came back to him and now he wondered if she was really ill, even delirious.

"I'm calling the doctor." He decided. "Just stay there." The phone was in the hall and he quickly looked on the card with the emergency numbers listed. After a short conversation he put the phone down.

"That was the centre, they're sending a paramedic out to look at you, but they don't know how long it will be."

"I'm ok I think." Her colour was coming back but she felt very weak.

He let her sit up but not stand.

"What are you scratching for?" She noticed his hand rubbing his arm.

"I'm not." It was only a slight irritation and he wasn't going to make a fuss about it. Probably the washing powder she used.

The thought messages had reached Bracket in a second as one of the observer cats had been prowling nearby and picked up a hostile presence. Mary's visitor had already been monitored and it was different to the one now marking the couple. Quickly a sentinel was despatched to June's house and learned that she had not been visited. This was strange.

But the only difference was that she had Wizard whereas the others didn't have pets.

There had been instances in The Paws' history where malevolent spirits would not go where another form resided. So did this current group not like cats? Hopefully the answer would be apparent soon.

June had been quite amused at the earlier antics. At first it had unnerved her a bit but Daphne's reactions had been quite entertaining. Her sister could easily rub her up the wrong way and didn't think before she spoke, not caring if she offended at all but got out of it by saying people couldn't take the truth. As she sat stroking Wizard, a smile crept over her face. She had taken the flack all these years, well maybe it was time for her to dish some out.

"Whatever it was, I will elaborate on it." She said to herself.

Wizard sat straight up and stared her in the face.

"What's up with you?"

The eyes were unflinching and he looked at her almost accusingly.

"But you don't like her." She continued.

He got off her lap and went to his favourite spot and stared at her.

"Look it's just a bit of fun." She explained. "It's my turn. See how she likes it. Might take her down a peg or two."

She felt quite smug and sat thinking as to the best way to put her plan into operation.

Although nothing had been detected at her house by way of the previous presence returning, something was growing by the minute that was alerting Wizard, and now Bracket was also aware. The seed of vengeance had been sown, would lay hidden for now and could not be destroyed but when activated fully could be more hazardous than any passing evil.

In view of Daphne's reaction and Ken's irritation, the observer cats were scanning the area for other similar seemingly minor ailments and what they found started to caused concern, for there was a wave of sudden such varying complaints springing up. The authorities started examining the water supplies, eating houses were tested for all aspects of hygiene but they seemed to draw a blank. Next people were asked to say if they had travelled abroad recently but that was inconclusive. Nobody seemed dangerously ill, but the population was generally unwell.

The evil power operating in the area was pleased with its results because this was all a distraction. While it was the main topic of attention and conversation, they were creeping in under cover to spread their own kind of epidemic. Control and possession. Many were already operating unbeknown to even their best friends. It could start very small with a simple request which then turned into an order, then a command. The weaker folk daren't stand up to the bullies even in their own family and before they knew it their lives were ruined.

The spirit cats knew all about this, having encountered it first hand and just when it seemed there was no way of overcoming it, some strange force took over until the bullies became the bullied. The Paws had their work cut out. It wasn't a case of taking out a group. The whole concept must be destroyed or it in turn would destroy the earth. For now they had to assimilate every single location before they could act but this would have to be alongside their other continual work of helping those in distress.

All except Marmaduke were out on assignments but were constantly aware of the latest detail. He had just finished a rather sad case but knew he couldn't dwell on it and must be ready for the next job whatever it was. Although they had all seen most things, there was always something that was different.
The alert called him to Canada to a homestead well away from its nearest neighbour. Viewing from afar he knew what must be done. The man was thrashing his wife with a leather

belt until her flesh bled. Instantly he called for helper cats to attend to the woman while he went for the man. As the strap was ripped from his hand the cat leapt, it was a very large cat. Marmaduke's orange stripes turned into the size of a tiger, its claws leaving distinct marks all over his body. The screams were ignored, as had his poor wife's been in the past. He wasn't killed. That would have put the woman in a volatile position, but he was left with evident marks of a wild animal attack.

Not even the helper cats saw Marmaduke, but all present received the tiger image so afterwards they would swear that's what was there. He left, his part of the job done knowing she would never again have to succumb to her husband's cruelty.

Most of the jobs Paws did were as instantaneous as this, for they did it and got out. The element of complete surprise coupled with the unknown foe seemed to work.

He returned to base fully aware of what each of the others was doing and the also the latest update on the villages.

Bonnet and Sunset were working together on what was becoming an all too familiar situation. This pair always had their attention on the vast number of retirement homes and sadly could have made it a full time job. For every resident that was treated with respect and kindness, the amount receiving abuse and loss of dignity way outnumbered them. But there was one at the moment which was about to have a shock.

The evening meal had finished and the staff, instead of letting the people settle and have a quiet time before going to bed, hustled them off to their rooms, gave them some medication and left them for the night. Any new or temporary staff were told to check them every so often but as they would all be asleep it didn't matter when. It was just a formality and something had to be put on the records. If the part time staff had been supplied by an agency, there was little chance of it happening for their idea was to let the regulars do the work and they were there simply because they had been sent and of course they would be paid.

One resident in particular at this home had caught The Paw's attention for it was June and Daphne's mother. She was getting on for eighty but appeared much older. Her skin was wrinkled and looked dried out, she had to be wheeled everywhere because her legs wouldn't hold her up, and most of the time she seemed far away, which was actually the effect of all the sedatives that were pumped into her. She was wearing incontinence pads which the staff changed when they remembered and often didn't bother to toilet her has they considered it a waste of time. By now her poor bottom was so sore but she couldn't complain.

The first thing Sunset asked was why did her daughters allow it but she knew the answer before the question arose. They didn't care. Neither wanted her in their own home and as long as she was being 'looked after' as they put it, she was almost forgotten. The only time they would take an interest would be when she passed to spirit and they could claim any money.

This kind of situation always made Bonnet angry.

"These are supposed to be decent people." She would rant. "And they don't even care for their poor mother. How callous is that?" The Paws were well aware that all old people haven't been nice in their early years and there is a thought that a few reap what they sowed, but they knew that Elsie, their mother had always been a caring loving person and didn't deserve this.

By way of easing her discomfort, Sunset had guided her soul to a beautiful place already so that she was free from the physical trauma but that didn't stop the two cats from carrying out their task. If they could save others from this hell hole it would be worth it. The more they saw of the place made them determined to expose the dreadful treatment for all to know, not only here but all the others like it.

Physically, Elsie was free from physical pain, but her spirit was still low. Caring angels were with her constantly as she hadn't completely gone through transition and was hovering almost half way between. She had been given the choice to proceed but her heart was heavy at the lack of love shown by her daughters. She had gone without when they were small so that they could eat and be clothed. Her husband had died young and she had brought them up herself, doing all sorts of work to bring in some money. And this was how they were content to leave her. She pondered what she had done wrong but couldn't find the answer, alright they weren't well off but she had given them all the love she could. Didn't that mean anything? No, she was determined not to make the last part of the journey until she had some kind of answer and called for help to let her find out.

It had to be discussed at length by the higher levels as they didn't want to put her at risk but knew she couldn't progress until her heart was at peace. She was in such a delicate state that the decision was made to let her have a little breathing space but must be constantly monitored and she must have a guardian in obvious presence at all times. Bonnet and Sunset were not directly involved in this but were storing all the facts for their own use.

Chapter 3

It was Sunday morning and Mary was getting ready for church. She had already been to early morning communion, had breakfast and got everything ready to cook for dinner for when she came back from matins.

The local church was never very full except on special occasions and all the regulars seemed to sit in their own preferred pew but not together so when it was time for a hymn, one could often feel they were singing alone. Some of the parishes were covered by one vicar now so the services were alternated between them. One would have matins one week and then evensong the next. A few with cars went to each but there weren't really enough to make much difference.

Mary had passed the time of day with one or two regulars and sat listening to the organ while waiting for the vicar to come out of the vestry. She was toying with the idea of sounding him out about what had happened to Daphne, without giving any names of course. She could just say 'a friend' but what if he thought she was talking about herself? She was still mulling it over when the small choir made their way to the stalls so the idea was put on hold.

She hadn't noticed the Reverend Simon Hughes was already at his place waiting to start the service. For the first time she realised he was quite an attractive man, must be a decade younger than her middle age years but still very tasty. Quickly she put the thoughts from her mind and tried to concentrate but found herself drawn to him constantly. Every minute of the service became torture as she felt feelings stirring inside her until it was as much as she could do not to fidget.

For a moment it seemed to ease. Unbeknown to her, a good spirit was pushing the evil power away, but it was too strong and reinforcements were called for but as soon as more good arrived it was doubled by the other side. If the reverend had only known what was going on inside the church, but he seemed oblivious to it. The higher levels observing this were baffled. Surely he must have picked up that something was wrong and fought it, but then they discovered something else, something frightening that needed immediate attention.

It was the vicar's body, and although his soul was in presence, it was gradually being overtaken by an evil substance. Although he was in full view of the congregation and choir, they were completely unaware of what was going on. And he still had his sermon to preach. Sentinels were despatched to all other churches in the region and told what to look for.

Mary was now beside herself. If this sensation didn't end soon she would be in danger of being in an embarrassing situation for her lower regions were building up ready to explode. Knowing the service as she did she knew there were at least twenty minutes still to go and she had to sit for a good fifteen of those looking at him in the pulpit. She was getting hot and her breathing was changing, she could feel herself panting and fought to stop it. It seemed to subside for a moment but as he climbed the steps to begin his sermon she started trembling.

He looked at her his eyes on fire and although he was speaking she didn't hear the words. Even when he looked around the other worshippers, she could feel his pull as though he had her on the end of a rope and was dragging her towards him. Frantically she started to wiggle her toes in her shoes, clenched her fists so tightly her nails dug into her palms and tried to breathe as deeply and slowly as she could. In fact all this was being controlled by several good spirits that had surrounded her. But the next second they had been dragged away and the evil was back.

This fight ensued until it was time for the last hymn and Mary couldn't wait to get out. As soon as she could, she rushed from the church even before Simon had chance to take up his position at the door, But if she thought that was the end of it, she was in for a shock.

Daphne and Ken seemed to have got over their minor ailments and hoped that was the end of it which physically it was, but the seed had been sown.

"So did you mean it, about not going over June's again?"

They had finished dinner and Ken had settled down to reading the paper and having a nap.

"Well, we'll have to see." Was the reply.

"Hmm." Was all Ken would offer but under his breathe muttered, "Women, always changing their bloody minds."

"What you going on about?" She snapped.

"Oh nothing." He knew it would get her going so he did it on purpose.

"If you've got something to say, you'd best come out with it, not chuntering to yourself."

"Well, you're like the wind. Depends which way it's blowing." He was quite enjoying this.

"Oh I see. Well, seeing as how I have to make all the decisions round here, I think I'm entitled." This was followed by a snort.

"Hmm. You make all the decisions do you?"

"I have to. I'd be waiting for ever before you'd raise yourself." She only took a breath then added "In more ways than one."

He slammed the paper down.

"And now what are you getting at?"

"You know very well. Call yourself a man."

His eyes blazed.

"Trust you to bring that up."

"Well it's more than you can." She spat the words at him.

He fired ready for his best shot.

"That's probably because of where it's going."

Her mouth fell open.

"You what?"

"You heard." He picked the paper up and gave her a knowing look.

"Are you saying I'm not worth making love to?"

He smirked.

"No I'm saying you're not worth shagging. Now do you get it?"

There was a stunned silence for a moment then she said quietly "I don't know what's come over you the last couple of days."

"Not commenting on that." He seemed to be wallowing in insulting her, something he'd never done.

Daphne left the room feeling quite down but after a few moments her fight returned and she stormed back, ripped the paper from his hands and faced him.

"Right Mr Big-I-Am. Things are going to change round here. Where the hell would you have been without me? I've worked my socks off to keep this place because we couldn't have managed on your money. I've brought up two kids, gone without luxuries, well let me tell you, no more. From now on I come first. I make the rules and if you don't like it, piss off and find someone else to shag as you like to call it. Get it?"

She turned and left him open mouthed, but felt a new surge of power and she liked it.

The evil onlookers clocked up two more conquests, for they had them both in their power now as well as Mary and the Vicar, and June was almost there. And this was only the pin point.

Ampersand already had the facts about Elsie and was in conference with Bonnet and Sunset. Unfortunately, this was only one case in thousands as for every elderly relative receiving love and care from their families, there were at least ten who seemed to have nobody. In some of the cases they had dealt with, they couldn't help but realise that the person concerned simply reaped what they had sown many years ago.

One particular man, in no way a gentleman, had treated his children so badly that they had grown up with no respect for him and would never entertain having him in their own home. They had done all they could by making sure he had gone into a decent residential care home and that was the end of it. As far as they were concerned, all of his money could go into his keep, they wanted none of it.

One of the staff tried to tell the daughter that she should take responsibility for him, after all he was old at which point the son in law almost marched the person into a side room and told his wife to take off her top. The carer's face went pale as she saw the scars all over the woman's back.

"That's what your dear old man did. He used to thrash her with a strap and threaten her that if she told anyone she would get more. I'm not going to ask her to show you any more, but her body is covered."

He gently put his arm round his wife then helped her to put her top back on. Then he hugged her.

The carer fled from the room in tears, and if anything, she had learned one very important lesson.

Elsie of course was the victim. She had done all she could for her family and needed the answers.

"Do you think it will ease her soul if she finds out?" Bonnet wondered.

"She was determined to know when I placed her with her guardians," Sunset answered then added "but it won't give her eternal peace, it's not what she wants to know."

Due to the way The Paws operated, the angels selected for the task would never have known who allocated the subject, they just accepted a soul had been placed in their care by a higher level.

The Paws had the information they needed but now the familiar question of whether to impart it or not had to be decided.

"Just the essential part of it?" Ampersand suggested.

"I don't think she'll settle for that." Bonnet thought. "With everything she is told, she will ask more questions."

Sunset was also wondering who would have to deliver the news.

"I think we could leave that to the guardians," Ampersand said "they do it all the time and you wanted to get to work on the home."

"And the others like it. It's never ending." Sunset agreed.

Bonnet summed it up. "Right, we send the knowledge to the guardians and they'll gently tell her that her daughters had their own lives and in short, that was what was more important to them."

"However they put it it's harsh for her." Sunset mused.

Ampersand asked "Will she be content to move on?"

"If it's adequate. Either way nothing will change." Bonnet summed up. "Unfortunately she will complete transition in a sad state."

They all knew what that meant. Elsie may not be at peace enough to proceed at the normal pace and could easily hover near her familiar surroundings, either seeking more answers or worse. She could turn on her daughters in her semi-permanent form, in other words she would be haunting them.

Bracket, although he often made light of some of the horrendous matters that he dealt with was very adept at sorting many serious situations. The other Paws respected his diligence and he would never give up until the case had been resolved to his satisfaction. He knew the evil power in the villages was spreading and was making its way into the smaller towns. The aim was to cause as much distrust, jealousy and callousness as possible which drew more into their flock followed by the promise of ridding people from the epidemic and returning them to their previous peaceful ways. It resembled the message "your computer has a virus, we can clear it for you, but at a price." Of course, this was a scam. Once people were under the evil spell, they were there for good, unless some almighty force could extract them before it was too late.

This was no new thing, it had been going on since man evolved upon the earth, but each time there was a new wave it seemed to be stronger and more possessive.

The changes that were being effected upon the likes of Daphne, Mary and the others were being duplicated all over the area. Some were having sexual desires upon the most unlikely people which in itself created unrest, others turned nasty and could fly into temper at any moment, and others used more underhanded methods, quietly stirring up trouble but never letting it be known that they were at the bottom of it. They could always find little pawns to do their dirty deeds and still go around with their heads held high.

Hashtag became involved quickly as he could pluck a piece of historic information out the air in a fraction of a second and immediately knew where the last such attack had taken place, where it started, who dealt with it and the end result.

All The Paws were on alert and paid special attention to even the slightest thing that seemed unusual, but at the same time carried on with their usual duties.

June was plotting. She wondered why she had always put up with her sister's obnoxious ways and not done anything about it.

"Well it's about time things changed around her," she said aloud "and we will see who thinks she is lady muck."

Something made her turn round. Wizard was staring straight through her.

"Stop that. I've told you before." She almost shouted.

He remained absolutely motionless for a moment, then slowly rose until he was standing, then even slower his back started to come up, the hair on end like a bottle brush.

"What the devil has got into you?" She was almost screaming at him.

"You called?"

The words were in her head and although she didn't actually hear them she might well have for they were as clear as if they had been shouted directly into her ear.

"Who's that?" It came out like a frightened scream and she jumped up.

Something pushed her back down into the chair.

"Don't worry about that. I'm here to help you." The voice was soft and sultry and definitely male and it had such a lulling effect that she listened without question.

"You want what is rightfully yours, and so you should." It continued.

"Time you weren't sat on. Time you stood up to the bullies."

The whisper came out "Yes. But I don't quite know how."

"Of course you don't. You aren't like that, but now is the time to change it all, to your advantage."

Was it her imagination or she could feel the form of a human shape pressing her down in her chair. She started to panic.

"I –I – I'm not sure what you mean."

"Oh you soon will be."

The caresses were getting a bit intimate now and she started to push whatever it was away.

"I'm leaving you now, but I will be back. Remember dear lady, I am your friend, I am here to see you get what you want."

As quickly as it started it had finished and she turned to look for Wizard but he had gone.

The temptation to intervene had to be dismissed. The male Paws knew that, harsh as it may seem, to move in now could frighten off whichever kind of evil this was, so they had to let it have its rein for a while in order to strike at the proper time. As soon as it had departed, June's guardian was alone with her but that was how it had to be. There was no good bringing in too many heavies just yet or they would know they were being tracked any would move elsewhere, then it all had to start again.

There was a knock at the door and Mary went to open it.

"Um, I think you dropped this in church."

She was surprised to see the vicar in the porch.

"Oh it's one of my bookmarks. Thank you for bringing it, I mean you needn't have come out of your way, it's very kind of you."

She was a little more than flustered and felt her lower parts throbbing.

"It was no trouble." Simon said and smiled, his gaze never wavering from her.

"I'm sorry, I mean, would you like a cup of tea?" She didn't know why she said it, it just came out.

"That would be very nice. Thank you."

She beckoned him into the small lounge saying "I'll put the kettle on." Then as an afterthought, "I won't be a moment."

"Please, don't worry, I did rather come unannounced." He too sounded a bit up tight.

"Oh please do sit down." She beckoned to one of the easy chairs as she went into the kitchen.

After a moment she returned "Won't be long." She was shaking but didn't know why.

"This is a lovely room." He tried to put her at ease but didn't know quite what to say himself.

"Thank you. You will have a piece of cake? It's home made."

"That sounds very nice."

"I've got lemon or chocolate sponge."

He smiled. "You know how to tempt a …. I mean I love lemon. That would be perfect."

Out of the two of them it would have been a job to decide who was the most nervous. Bracket would have been quite amused except that he knew there was something not right about it. They were both being played like puppets and when it went too far and the rumour went round the village, the vicar would be shamed and Mary would be branded a loose woman. Something that would plague them for the rest of their lives and it would get out because the evil would see to it. Just one of the many tricks always used on the unsuspecting yet couldn't be dismissed.

Both had managed to drink their tea without spilling it and eat the cake without it either breaking up or crumbs going all over the place. It was almost a relief when Mary took the tray into the kitchen and relaxed a little.

"I take it they are your parents." Simon pointed to the photos on the sideboard.

"Yes and that one is of my grandparents although I don't remember them." She was much more at ease now.

As she sat in the chair facing him she was drawn to his lovely smile and didn't notice his eyes were almost boring into her, his attention on her breasts which didn't show much under her loose blouse but he was right on target. He crossed his legs and she was getting the urge to do the same.

"You know you can always confide in me," he whispered softly, "anything you say will go no further."

"Oh, yes, well I know that." She was at a loss for words. It seemed a funny thing to say. Why would she want to confide…..? Then it hit her. He must know. "I mean……"

"Yes? Something you feel you have to tell me, about the service for instance?"

She blushed.

"No, no certainly not, I mean, why would there be just because Daphne…. Oh, No, there isn't anything." She had rambled and nearly let out a secret, something she had never done. What had got into her?

He got up from his chair and she quickly did the same. The next minute he was in front of her holding her in his arms and she was responding.

The force being used was too strong for either of them to resist and the longer it lasted, the more they wanted from each other. These two were now under the control of the evil powers and would have no will of their own but could perform any disgusting intimate act they were ordered to do. Again The Paws dare not intervene at this stage or it could have jeopardised the final outcome. They had been in this situation too many times. Hopefully they could do a cleansing ritual at a later stage but that was not on the programme for now.

With normal groups or families, if one person went missing or seemed withdrawn, the others, if they were caring would ask if they were alright. With The Paws it was different. Whether together or apart, each knew what the other was doing so when Hashtag had now put himself into a withdrawal mode, it was understood he was working on something that took all his concentration, but the rest knew all the details. Sometimes they could even press the 'off' button so that their vibes didn't interfere with his point of attention. Although no power could ever trace back to them, there were times when a calm atmosphere was called for in order to execute a particular plan and avoid the slightest suspicion.

His attention was on three points of the earth. Two were in North America, but the third was only a few miles from the villages. Somehow they were connected but it wasn't evident at this moment. The one thing all The Paws were aware of was that it wasn't a low level evil, but appeared to be one of the highest they had ever encountered. This time it seemed to be aimed at the soul regardless of the host. The first instinct was to draw in extra protection on all living species but somehow Hashtag knew that they had to identify which particular form was involved. Surely not every living thing was in danger.

Switching themselves off from his thoughts Marmaduke conferred with the others.

"It could be chance but this is evolving at the same time as the evil we've been monitoring. Either perfect timing to drain resources, or neither know what the other is planning."

All were in agreement and it was decided that Marmaduke would keep himself free for when Hashtag was ready to come out of his concentration period and meanwhile the rest could continue with tasks in hand.

Bonnet and Sunset agreed it was time for Elsie to move, one way or the other and after doing an instantaneous scan of her they had the answer. The message was relayed to the caring angels to give her the basic facts as gently as possible. As usual they took the orders without question knowing it was from a high authority.

It had been decided to bring her late husband into play with the hope it might sway her to go with him rather than return but the choice would be hers.

As they moved him into her area, her heart leaped. Again she was the lovely young woman who had fallen for this gentle loving lad and as they now met, all her sadness left her for a moment and the years were wiped away. Slowly she realised that she must have died to be seeing him this way but the guardian explained why she had been kept in the safe area.

"You won't stay here Elsie, you have a choice. You can return to your body for a short period if you have anything you need to do, or you can go with your husband now."

It didn't take long for her to decide.

"I want to go please but can you tell me why our daughters abandoned me when I needed them?"

"If you won't go without an answer Elsie, we will tell you but you may feel a little hurt."

"I feel I know. I've been thinking." She answered. "They didn't need me any more did they? They have their own lives." Then added "And short memories."

"That's about it Elsie." The reply was very soft.

Her husband took her in his arms.

"But I want you my love as much as I ever did. I've been waiting for you."

She reached out to the angels.

"Thank you for looking after me. I'm ready."

They had never left her all through her life but like many people she never knew.

Sunset was satisfied for now but both she and Bonnet knew that when Elsie had rested she could easily seek revenge. It was very common even in the nicest people.

The phone call came as no surprise to Daphne and as she relayed the news to June she suggested they both go together to collect the belongings. The younger sister felt a slight pang of guilt.

"We should have gone to see her more often Daph. She was our Mum."

"What, go to that stinking rat hole, not on your life."

"It was horrid."

Daphne got straight down to brass tacks.

"Well I'll sort the will out and we can use what bit she's got left."

"Don't suppose it's much, the home took enough."

"Oh they didn't know everything."

"What?" For some reason June began to get suspicious.

"Well, if you've got over a certain amount, you have to pay more if you get what I'm saying. Well she hadn't."

"But her house was sold." June was really wondering just what had been going on.

"Well it doesn't pay to let others get their mitts on your hard earned cash."

"I'm not quite sure I follow you Daph."

She was cut off with a brusque "It will be fine, you'll see. Anyway we will have to go down as soon as we can because they need the room."

As June put the phone down, she had serious doubts as to her sister's actions. As she turned she nearly fell over Wizard who was sitting on the floor staring at her.

"Oh, move, what a silly place to sit."

His eyes held her gaze and his whole being seemed to be emitting a warning.

"It's alright little man." She went to pick him up but he turned and walked away flicking his tail as he went. At the kitchen door he stopped, turned and again fixed his eyes on her for a moment then returned to his favourite place.

Whatever he was trying to say, it put a serious doubt in her mind as to what Daph was playing at, but one thing was for sure, she was going to find out, no matter what it took.

Chapter 4

The Reverend Simon Hughes was on his knees praying for all he was worth about this recent transgression. He didn't know what had made him succumb to feelings he knew he shouldn't experience. Never before had anything like that happened. Of course as a young man he had felt the attraction to the ladies but had put it out of his mind as he had dedicated his life and soul to the Lord. He knew other clergy married but his decision was made from the start to remain a bachelor and that's how it would always be.

Now in his early forties he was a fairly attractive man and quite a few had set out their stall for him only to be disappointed. But now to have made physical contact with a lady of about his own age was unthinkable. But that wasn't the only problem. He was wrong, but had thoroughly enjoyed it and wanted more, in fact he couldn't wait until the next time he saw her, but what would her reaction be? The desperate feeling was affecting him just thinking about her and prayers or not, he got up, went into the bathroom and relieved himself, which meant he would have to go and confess to that as well.

The evil knew they had him. That was easier than they imagined but it didn't diminish the conquest, because if they got him they could get others. It wouldn't stop with insatiable lust, in a short time they would add possession and if anyone so much as looked at her he would be on to them. She would love the attention at first but soon she would feel taken over and realise she had no will power of her own. But by then it would be too late. The fact that they had destroyed two good lives would only add to the success and with its hold firmly planted, the evil would continue to spread.

Elsie had long gone before her offspring showed up at the home.

The manager had already cleared the room much to the annoyance of the sisters who wanted to go through their Mum's personal possessions.

"I do think you could have had the decency to let us gather her things together." Daphne stated.

"Money love, someone was waiting for the room, had to get it emptied and cleaned." The manager wanted to get them out of the way as soon as possible.

Daphne was standing looking down at the woman.

"In that case, you owe us money." She snapped.

"How do you make that out?"

Daphne got out her diary.

"We paid to the end of the month. That's another ten days away. You will be charging some other person from now I would guess."

The manager wasn't pleased at being in this position.

"Well of course you pay from the day you take occupancy." She snorted.

"So you mean she's charging for the same room twice?" June was getting the gist of it now.

"She knows that's exactly what she's doing. Now Lady, you owe us for ten days." Daphne folded her arms in defiance.

The manager smirked.

"No I don't, and before you say any more, Elsie paid for her room not you, so I don't owe you a penny."

"But I have Power of Attorney, I paid her bills." The attitude was 'got you'.

"No difference. It came from her bank. We can only pay back to the same account, only of course that will be frozen now won't it."

"Well, I am handling her affairs, so you will pay it to me so that I can settle her estate."

"Oh?" A smirk came over the woman's face. "Not got a solicitor then?"

"I don't see that's any of your business. You owe Elsie's estate money and I am damned sure you are going to pay it."

"Get a lawyer to put it in writing. Can't do anything without the proper authorisation. Rules you know."

Her tone was really beginning to rankle the sisters and it was June who replied "Very well, you will have one, and you will also be exposed for extortion. And we want to check Mum's clothes and possessions, here in front of you before we leave."

Even Daphne was taken aback at this unexpected outburst, and it did seem to subdue the manager somewhat at the thought of a solicitor being brought in, however she retained her outward appearance of annoyance.

"They're here, well most of them." The woman pushed a black waste sack towards them. "Now I'm busy so take that and let me get on. I do have other people to see to you know."

"Hold it right there madam." Daphne's arm came out. "When we have checked."

June was already taking things out of the bag and laying them on the floor.

"Where's her dressing gown?" She demanded.

"That? Oh we gave it to Rosie upstairs, she hadn't got one. Elsie wouldn't have minded."

Daphne barred the door so that this creature couldn't get out until they were done.

"Her watch? It's not here." June nearly exploded.

"It was." Was all she got by way of an explanation.

"Well it isn't now. Daphne you check."

Without taking her eyes off the manager, Daph moved over to the array now spread on the carpet.

"I can't see it. Can you see it?" She was seething.

"We can't oversee everything you know."

Daphne bent over the desk and fumed "The basic rule is to take care of patient's property, valuables should be locked away in a safe!"

There was a shrug. "I didn't clear it."

How long this would have gone on no one could have guessed but there was a knock on the door and one of the carers said the manager was needed immediately. With no alternative they had to take the belongings and go, but they wondered if the interruption had been timed so that they couldn't linger any longer than the manager wanted.

As they drove away they both knew this wasn't the end of the matter but the worst was yet to come and it would be nothing to do with the home's shortcomings.

Hashtag's findings were being discussed by the group. Having confirmed that the evil cells working the three areas were all from the same kind of sect, he then found that the one local to the villages had a connection with the North Americas ones through families that had emigrated years before. Now it was beginning to tie together. This was no random attack but one which must have been carefully planned either for revenge against the living but possibly also aimed at the departed. The earthlings would not be the ultimate goal but just a means of connecting all parties involved.

Marmaduke was looking at all the recent developments. What had started as a passing visit at June's had then spread to her sister, onto her friend Mary then drawn the vicar into the plan. Sunset then brought in Elsie's passing and was sure that had to have some part in it. Hashtag was in agreement but pointed out that they should be trying to pre-empt the next move for this was only the tip and it wasn't obvious how deep it went. He said he would examine the American side in more detail as there had to be a history of events which was now causing this reaction. Bracket offered to take one source and Ampersand the other then Hashtag could pool their findings and make his comparison to which he agreed. It was also decided that Bonnet should watch the sisters as something fishy was going on there leaving Sunset to deal with the home and also monitor Elsie's progress.

It was Wednesday afternoon and Mary had just been to the local shop on her way home from work. As she went in the front door she noticed an envelope on the mat. She picked it up and rather bemused took it into the kitchen and put it on the table with her bag while she put the kettle on. It merely said 'Mary' on the envelope and as she opened it a handwritten letter slid out. Putting on her reading glasses she began to read the words aloud.

Dear Mary,
I feel I must apologise for my unseemly conduct. I do hope you can forgive me, there is no excuse, it was very wrong of me.
Yours sincerely
Simon Hughes

It was written on plain paper, not the vicarage letterheads but did have his phone number at the top almost as though he was inviting her to contact him. Without thinking, she picked up the phone and dialled the number shaking with excitement.
"The Reverend Hughes speaking."
"Oh, Hello this is Mary." She was quivering all over.

"Mary! It is so good of you to ring, I didn't thing you would, I mean I hoped you would but......"

"I had to." She cut in. "You didn't do anything wrong, and I was equally guilty."

It went very quiet.

"Are you there Simon?"

"Yes. I am a very lucky man. You are being very understanding." His voice was shaking.

"I'm just making some tea." She almost whispered. "Would it be wrong of me to ask you to join me?" Her words came out slowly but her brain was yelling 'please do.'

"I would be more than pleased. And thank you again."

His mind was churning. Although he had always planned to be unmarried, maybe this lady had been put in his path for a reason. They were both single and as a couple they could understand better when parishioners had problems. She would make the ideal vicar's wife, gentle and kind and not as open as some he could mention. He realised she may not be quite all that bright but that gave her a pure quality in his eyes. So he estimated that maybe she had been sent from God, but it never entered his head that they were being pushed together from the other source and for a totally different reason.

It seemed to take an age before she heard the gentle tap on the front door. As her small house was set back a little from the road, the door was not one you would see just passing by which afforded a little privacy, and as he had come on foot there was no car parked there.

Her smile as she opened the door reassured him that he hadn't offended her, in fact she was beaming.

"Thank you for coming, I didn't think you would, and it was a little forward of me to ask." She was agitated partly from nerves, but more as the sight of him sent her pulses racing, besides other things.

"I was so pleased you asked."

He stood in front of her and simultaneously they were in each others arms, his lips pressed on hers. As he wasn't wearing his cassock, it wasn't long before something else was pressing against her causing her to squirm uncontrollably.

"We mustn't." She whispered but did nothing to pull away.

"It wouldn't be fitting." He agreed between kisses.

"I can't believe it's happening to me, it must be a dream." Her eyes were tightly closed.

"Well if it is, I'm a big part of it." He caressed her ears, neck and shoulders slowly letting his hand slide down her chest.

"Should we all be watching this?" The Paws were picking up on what was happening regardless of their other duties.

"We could miss something important." Bracket offered as an excuse but was reminded by Marmaduke that they were not acting as voyeurs.

"Oh well, that's alright then." Ampersand seemed satisfied but the tone had the hint of a mock in it which didn't go unnoticed.

Both Simon and Mary were lost in the moment and just followed their overpowering instincts, unable to stop or even think about what they were doing. It seemed so natural that neither felt embarrassed afterwards when it was cleaning up time. They knew from that point there was no going back. They were together and always would be, or so they believed.

"Be a shame to pour cold water on it." Bracket thought.

"Oh, they'll get that soon enough and nothing could even get through to them at the moment."

Hashtag was being very matter of fact but Marmaduke reminded them all that they were not allowed to intervene at the present. It just had to take its inevitable course, however heartbreaking that might be.

Although Mary had heard the news about Elsie and had offered her condolences, she hardly knew the woman so it didn't have much effect on her and she had other things on her mind.

But Daphne and June had work to do. After getting all the necessary paperwork sorted, the funeral had to be arranged. Everything seemed to present a problem.

"Where would the lady be going from?"

Neither wanted her to go from the home and it didn't seem right for her to go from either of their homes as she hadn't lived there. So she was to go from the funeral directors, they would return there for a cup of tea afterwards. Again, neither sister wanted the bother of providing a buffet. There wouldn't be many mourners, Elsie's brother and sister had long gone as had her few friends. Someone from the home was forced to come, so apart from them and Ken and the vicar, it would be very sparse. As it was only going to be a very short service at the crematorium, they were lucky to get a slot on Thursday the following week.

"I'll be glad when it's all over." Daphne said in not too quiet a voice as they left the undertakers.

"It will come out of her money." June was checking, not asking a question.

"It will have to." Was the short reply.

"I'll be interested to see her bank book." June made her way to her car. She was giving Daphne a lift as Ken was at work.

"You living in the dark ages? You don't have bank books now."

"Well, whatever it is. A statement or something."

Daphne took a deep breath. "We've got to take the death certificate in and send some to goodness knows how many more places. I don't think you realise June just what has to be done in times like this, and I could do without it."

"And how do you think I coped when Jack died. I had it all then."

Daphne looked out of the window and sniffed.

"Yes well we were on holiday then. We could hardly come back could we, not with what it cost."

June had an opening here.

"Yes I often wondered how you managed it."

"Managed what?" Daphne turned now.

"Well you have always said about how wonderful it was, and how much it cost. Must have been a hefty loan."

There was silence for a moment and June knew she had a foothold but she didn't want to be driving when she faced her with her suspicious. There must be no distractions.

Marmaduke could see a pattern forming and they all agreed that a lot of family skeletons were about to come out of the closet both in England and North America, for one cell was in the USA and the other in Canada.

"Money." They all chorused. It all had to go back maybe a century but it was certain that money or possessions had instigated a family feud that didn't end with the death of those involved but was still boiling on other levels. There must be a relationship running through it all but what had started as a family quarrel had escalated into something so bitter, the evil element was to the fore, hence the greed, control and possession along with acute jealousy had manifested into a living thing that could destroy anything in its path, not physically, but mentally.

Sunset lost no time in getting back to her task and although a few minor incidents came up she quickly sorted those and could now concentrate on the retirement home, plus any others being run in the same disgusting way.

First she had to check on Elsie and found that although out of her physical trauma, her spirit was far from settled. The angel guardians who were trying to help her progress peacefully knew this poor soul wouldn't rest until she knew justice had been done, or she had got her answers for she seemed to be searching for something.

Sunset picked up their thought waves and turned her concentration on the home. It didn't take her long to learn that, not only were the residents being neglected as far as their care went, but they were also being abused. Several bore the bruises of being handled roughly and more than a few had actually been hit if they didn't respond. They were drugged at night so that they caused the staff no bother and it was rare for them to be regularly checked, but the record forms were all filled in as though they had.

The abominable care was only part of it. When checks were done by the care company, all the books were in perfect order, that is all that was entered into the ledgers, but what wasn't listed was providing a nice little income for the manager and one or two that she needed to ensure kept the mouths shut. Sunset didn't have to examine every page or every computer audit trail, she knew from an instantaneous scan what was going on. Every resident and their families were being well and truly fleeced. Apart from the fraud, what concerned her most was the indignity the poor things were having to suffer.

Time the blow the lid on this and every other home in the same situation, but this would not be done with any physical evidence. The Paws didn't need that, they had their own ways.

Ampersand was happy to cover the Canadian cell while Bracket studied the American one. They could have been at extreme ends of the continent but one was only over the border at Niagara with the other in Pennsylvania and with the Paws' skills one could almost have monitored both simultaneously, but even in the spirit world and with their talents they still accepted that two working together may just pick up on a tiny detail the other may not. They were never complacent.

It came as no surprise to Hashtag to find that the two evil cells were connected although they did not communicate, but it quickly became apparent that there was no tie to the sisters or their family and this seemed strange as all three were identical in the way the evil was manifesting itself and spreading through contacts.

Ampersand even found that a local middle aged spinster had been taken under the wing of a passing preacher man. She lived in a small hick town and had been swept along by his promise to put herself in his hands and she would be given eternal salvation. Well, he wasted no time in giving it to her as often as he could. She had even heard beautiful music at one point.

"No that's just an orgasm dear." Ampersand couldn't help thinking.

She was keen to know if Bracket had experienced the same, but quickly corrected that to 'observed a similar incident'. He confirmed that, although not identical it bore the trademark almost in reverse. This time a priestess from the Angels of Song community had shown a local bachelor the way to atone for his sins, although he couldn't think for the life of him what sins. But it was a very pleasurable way to reach heights he never had before and so he couldn't see any reason to question it.

What Bracket knew was that when the travelling church moved on, the man would not be going with them and would have to seek new ways satisfying this new found happiness, but that was yet to come.

Hashtag now had to find some way to connect these two cells whilst staying alert for any new ones popping up. Of course the earth was littered with such activities which would have made it almost impossible for the novice spirit to make any sense of it, but The Paws were extreme in their talents.

As Daphne had declared she wouldn't go to June's again, she insisted that if June had anything to get off her chest, she should come to her. Ken had wanted to go for a drink that evening so the sisters decided to tag along as it seemed the only way they could talk without being on the phone.
"Well I think I should know everything you're up to." June got quickly to the point.
"What is there to know? And what do you mean by up to. I'm not up to anything." Daphne repeated the wording as she didn't really know how to answer.
June lowered her voice as much as possible.
"You know very well what I mean. You're being very cagey about all Mum's money and I want to know. It's my right after all."
"Well this isn't the place to discuss it." Daphne almost slammed her empty glass down on the table.
"But you won't talk about it when I ask. Why not? What are you hiding?"
She couldn't help but notice that Ken seemed to be getting very uneasy. He was fidgeting with his glass and kept looking round the bar as if waiting for someone.
"I wonder if anyone's up for a darts match."
His words were ignored and he kept glancing at his wife.
"What's up with you Ken?" June came right out with it.
"Me? Oh no I'm ok."

That was enough. June finished her drink, grabbed her bag and got to her feet.

"Well you've had your chance. If you won't come clean and own up to what you've been scheming, I'll put it in the hands of somebody who will find out for me."

"No wait." Daphne' tried to grab her but wasn't quick enough.

June bent over just out of arms reach and mouthed "And Mum's money will pay for it."

With that she left.

The two were left in stunned silence. Daphne pushed her glass towards Ken and almost whispered "I need another drink."

While he was away she was mulling everything over. In her mind she had done what she thought was for the best, but would her sister understand?

While it was clear as anything to the Paws what had happened, it was only just dawning on June but she needed a poke in the right direction. As soon as she got home she felt the need to sit in her chair and go over things on her own before she made her next move, oblivious to the fact that Sunset was about to feed her valuable information.

She closed her eyes and the thoughts floated through her brain. Although her husband had left her enough to be comfortable, she had needed to stay at work to maintain their standard of living. It wasn't posh but they had the things they wanted and enjoyed going out. They had only had one child, a boy who had left home to take a job elsewhere and kept in touch now and then. She never had been very sure what he did and he seemed to move from one place to another. No amount of questions provided an answer and he often fobbed them off with 'the firm is sending me to France next week' and he gave the impression it was to do with time share properties.

June's employer had been very understanding after the death of Elsie but she knew she had to return until the funeral, and then she would need that day off.

All this swept through her mind, quickly summing up her own circumstances and then her thoughts turned to Daphne. What a difference. She had decided a few years ago that work was too much for her, although she only did a few hours a day. But that didn't seem to change their lifestyle in fact --- she stopped as Sunset let the truth hit her. They seemed better off. They had bought a new car and always went abroad for their holidays. The explanation was that Ken had won on the lottery, and although June didn't expect anything it did just occur to her that she had never been invited to join them and her sister never asked if she was alright financially.

The next bolt was delivered immediately.

"It was just after Mum went into the home!" She almost yelled. "They were using her money while I carried on fending for myself." But then her anger came to the surface.

"But it wasn't their's to have. It was Mum's. They were robbing her." Then straight away "And me!"

The steam was nearly coming out of her ears and she admonished herself for being so blind. But now she really had the ammunition and she was going to fire it.

Picking up the phone she dialled the number. It was answered after a few rings.

"Hello?" Daphne sounded as though she was expecting this.

"Daphne," June stated in a very firm tone "when I finish work tomorrow, I will be coming round to see you, please be there."

"Now look June, there's no good getting all excited, we're all upset you know."

"Oh I'm not excited. About four o'clock. I'll see you then." With that she put the phone down.

"She's coming round straight from work tomorrow." A rather subdued Daphne told Ken.

"Well I can't say I'm surprised. Didn't take much working out. Thought she might have twigged before though."

"You'll have to be here." She announced.

"I'll still be at work. Put her off till I'm home or better still, sort it yourself."

He got up and left the room muttering to himself "I knew it, I told her."

Sunset had the whole picture as far as this family were concerned and on earth it remained to be seen whether there would always be a feud, or in fact they put the past behind them and said no more about it, but that was not going to happen. Apart from finding out she'd been cheated, June would feel stupid at not having seen it before.

But whatever the sisters decided would not satisfy Elsie. In her supposedly resting state she was demanding to know everything. The previous fob off hadn't worked and she knew instinctively there was much more going on that she had been led to believe. The guardians knew she would never be at peace until she discovered the truth, but then would she rest or try to take the matter into her own hands?

Chapter 5

It was becoming increasingly obvious to the village that the vicar was visiting Mary more than some of the gossip mongers considered necessary. A couple of them were in the village shop exchanging the latest suppositions, and as usual for them were adding things on in an attempt to be the one with the juiciest titbits. The owner wasn't much better and as soon as one tasty morsel reached her ears it came out of her mouth at the first opportunity.

"Well, I've seen him going there every day." One stated.

"Must be sinful if she needs that much solving." Was the reply.

"Don't you mean absolving?" The owner corrected.

There was a sniff. "Well whatever he's giving her."

This was met with a titter.

"And we all know what that is."

"She looks different."

"I know just what you mean. She's fairly glowing she is."

"Ah, he's pushed his boat up her river, you mark my words."

"Don't seem right do it?"

The owner wanted to elaborate so said "Well, they are both free, as far as we know, unless you know something we don't."

"Oh no I was just saying."

There was a pause so it was obvious nothing else was forthcoming and they seemed to have hit a dead end.

"I'm doing the flowers with her this weekend!"

The other two looked at the woman.

"Oooh. So you'll be able to quiz her, round about sort of."

"More than that. I shall keep my eyes peeled if he turns up. You know what I mean?"

There were nudges and snorts all round as this offered to be the source for the next discussion.

As there seemed to be no other gossip worth mentioning, the two left with a promise to let the owner know the minute they learned anything new.

If they had been privy to the phone call going on at that moment their tongues would have wagged right out of the shop. Although it had only been a short time, Simon and Mary were getting closer by the minute and could hardly wait until the next time they saw each other. Although he was trying to be as discreet as possible, net curtains were twitching and even mobile phone were pointed in their direction to try and grab them in a compromising position. But they were a bit too clever for that and never gave any show of affection in public. But as one of the women in the shop had noticed, Mary certainly was changing even since the Sunday service when she looked her normal uninteresting self. And as all this had happened in a few days, there were rumours that it must have been going on without people noticing.

Mary felt she was floating on air. It was like a fairytale and she hoped that she wouldn't wake up one morning and it had all been a dream.

The Paws were aware that the evil in the area had a great part to play in this affair and it seemed to be centred round the three women, and the vicar. Up to now it had flitted around as if sifting out which parties to use and which to discard. The theory that it would drag as many as possible into its net faded into the background for it had made its selection and would now set to work. This was nothing new. A force had been known to sweep an area seemingly taking everything with it, sometimes infecting the whole area in its bid for supremacy, but as in the present situation it would then handpick its players, often pre selected for whatever reason.

Most groups would have wondered why the vicar was on the list. Lesser evils believed if they could corrupt a holy man it was a step up for them, but The Paws, weighing up the whole scene knew this was not the case as a pattern was forming.

June was at Daphne's front door at 4 o'clock. She only had to knock once and as soon as the door opened marched in and stood waiting for Daphne to close the door and they went into the lounge and sat down.

"Right you know why I'm here, so don't let's have any silly business."

June forthrightness knocked her sister back a bit and she didn't like it.

"Well as I said," she began "I'm the one who's had to deal with everything regarding Mum and I did what I considered at the time was in her best interests."

"Which was?"

"Perhaps it would be better if we waited until Ken was home." Daphne was playing for time.

June took as deep breath. "You've just said you were the one who had to deal with everything. So you don't need Ken here to back you up." The tone was very curt now.

Her sister was taking charge and she was determined not to let her get the better of her.

"Yes I did, because you didn't offer to help did you? Oh no, where were you when everything had to be sorted out to get her into a home. Off in a caravan on the east coast." Daphne fired her words like a bullet.

"Yes and that had been booked a long time, so it was strange that you should pick that exact time to move Mum when you knew I was only away for a week, which was all I ever got."

"She had to go when they said there was a room or we would have lost it." Daphne was emphatic.

"We could go on like this all day, which is probably what you're working on," June popped in to let it be known she could see that Daph was playing for time, "so let's get to the point. What exactly did you do with all Mum's money?"

"Well there wasn't all that much in her bank." Daphne stated.

"Until her house was sold." June finished it off for her.

"And that took ages. You wouldn't have realised all that had to be done."

"No." June said very slowly. "Especially clearing the house."

"Well you couldn't expect me to do that as well, not with all the paperwork that had to be sorted out. Anyway Ken helped you."

June was silent for a moment then came in with the punch.

"This still isn't explaining what you did with her money. So tell me, and tell me in detail. What did you do with it?" She couldn't be any more forthright and stared at her sister for the reply.

"I've tried to tell you. If they found out how much Mum had after the house was sold, she would have been charged the earth to go into residential care."

"And you of course, looking after our future interests couldn't allow that." June was trying not to get too far ahead until she had dragged the facts out.

"Exactly. Now you understand." Daphne was relieved.

"Not for one tiny moment."

"Well it's obvious, you'd have done the same in my position."

"Done what?" June had her backed into a corner.

"Well what do you think? You're not that stupid surely."

"It's not what I think. It's what you did. Something you aren't too keen to admit. So that makes it illegal."

Daphne fumed. "It wasn't illegal at all, it was no more than businessmen do everyday. They are always moving money around from one account to the other."

"Ah. So there we have it. You were laundering it."

"What?"

"Dirty word? You should have thought of that before Daph."

"Look I only moved some so that she hadn't got the amount where they could charge, at least not a lot."

June gave a sickly smile.

"Let me rephrase that for you dear." The air was vibrating. "You moved the lot into your own bank account, probably where you creamed the interest as well."

"You think I would do that?"

It was mock horror and June knew it.

"I don't think, I know and it can be proved."

At that moment the door opened and Ken came in from work.

"Oh, sorry, I'll go and….."

"No need Ken." Daphne beckoned him in gratefully, now she had an ally. Turning back to June she hissed "Now you can make your accusations, I have a witness."

Ken looked uneasy "I'd rather not if you don't mind."

If Daphne was going to try and change his mind she was beaten to it.

"No Ken don't' go, I'd be very interested in what you have to say. We'd just got to the point where your lovely wife had moved all Mum's money into her own bank account."

He looked from one to the other and being outnumbered thought it better to do as he was told so sat in one of the chairs.

Daphne made sure she was first to speak.

"Well you've got that wrong young lady. I always made sure there was enough in her bank to pay the monthly bit we had been told about."

"So let me get this straight. It was moved into yours to gain interest, they you moved some back each month for them to take by direct debit. I'm going on what the manager said about it coming out of her account. Now do correct me if I'm wrong." The sarcasm was dripping off every word.

"Well it made good sense. Why should they have it all?"

Ken was shifting about so much Daphne was distracted.

"If you need the toilet for goodness sake go and stop wriggling like that."

"I don't." He looked even more awkward.

June smiled sweetly at him.

"So Ken. What's your version?" As the question was delivered her face changed to that of an inquisitor.

"I – I um." Was all he could manage.

June turned back to Daph. "Got your puppy dog well trained."

Daphne opened her mouth to speak but June was quicker.

"And perhaps you can explain where the new car came from, just after Mum was admitted. And perhaps you can explain how you suddenly managed to go on all those foreign holidays."

She had left herself wide open for she knew they would say it was from a lottery win, but some instinct, thanks to spiritual help, made her stand her ground.

"Ha." Daphne smirked now. "Ken won the lottery so get out of that one."

"Oh yes the lottery. The bank audit trail will show that one. Remind me just how much was it Ken?"

Her tone made him feel she already knew and before his wife could intervene he had come out with what June was waiting for.

"Ten pounds."

The air was blue as Daphne hit the roof but what came next was and even greater shock.

"Tell her." He yelled. "Tell your sister what you made me do."

"Shut up you stupid fool."

June was almost afraid to ask but she knew it was essential she had the whole picture.

Ken looked straight at her ignoring Daphne.

"She made me invest some of it to make even more money."

At first that didn't seem too bad until he continued.

"But it didn't work."

June took a deep breath.

"Go on."

"It all went wrong. We lost thousands. If your Mum hadn't died when she did, we couldn't have paid anything for her keep."

Nobody could have said how long the silence went on. Ken was ashamed but glad he had spoken for it had been driving him to despair. Daphne sat stone faced, angry at him for admitting it. June seemed to be the only one who's brain was working.

"Right. I shall inform my solicitor and also the fraud squad because what you have done is illegal." She wasn't sure but had the front to say it to scare the poo out of them.

"But I had Power of Attorney." Daphne cut in.

"Even worse, because you weren't acting in her interests but using it for your own ends. Right. I will get an estimate of what her assets should have been, deduct any monies paid to the home, and funeral costs, and you will owe me half of the net figure."

"We will do no such thing." Daphne started but saw June's face and realised for the first time that she was in deadly earnest.

As she stood up to go, June added "And there will be a court order to make you pay it. I don't care if you both have to work for the rest of your lives."

With that she let herself out of the front door leaving them in a stunned silence.

"Where did all that come from?" She asked herself as she drove home knowing there was little chance of her getting anything but she would see a solicitor, of that she was certain.

Unbeknown to her, Jack sat beside her punching the air.

"That's my girl." He thought as he blew her a kiss.

But he wasn't the only witness. Elsie had fought her guardians to let her visit her offspring for that was the only way she was going to learn the truth. Jack had been aware of her presence but she had brushed him aside because this was something she had to do alone.

"If only I could have done a bit of eavesdropping while I was still alive," she fumed "then things would have been different."

"So what was stopping you?" One angel put it to her.

"How could I? I wasn't dead then, you only do this when you're gone."

They could have explained that her spirit had been ongoing and if she had tuned in she would have had the same results as she had now but earthly matters blind the inner eye. But she was not in the right frame of thought to take that on as well, so they knew they had to let it run its course until she had all her answers. Unfortunately for them it was not love that was driving her, it was hatred and revenge built out of disappointment and the feeling of being abandoned and it was gathering momentum by the minute.

She was disappointed in them both, obviously Daphne's greed and illegal actions were one thing, but she knew there was more to sweet little June than most people realised.

Sunset had set many traps. She knew which retirement homes were abusing the residents and was ready for the kill. As we know The Paws have the skill to let people, whether in body or totally in spirit, think what they want them to think. So when messages appeared in various authorities' inboxes, they did the usual check to see if they were scams, but knew that they had to take enough action in case there was any truth in it. It only took a few surprise calls on a few homes to realise that someone had blown the whistle. The disgusting state that the elderly were kept in began to hit the headlines and soon every home was being thoroughly checked and the staff investigated. Only when Sunset was satisfied that dignity, hygiene and general well being was on the way to be resumed did she return to other duties.

Many earthlings got a pat on the back for their diligence, but strangely enough, no one could find the original messages that had started the investigation. That was something for which there would never be an answer.

The Paws although still monitoring the daughters and Mary, were comparing notes on the North America cells. All three bore similar patterns and were not connected in any way to other evil entities. So whatever was going on was confined to these three venues alone. There had to be a family or friend element but at the moment it was very well hidden.

Ampersand was the first to dig up something which may have some bearing. It was quite by accident when she was admiring the black squirrels at Niagara that she noticed something unusual under a tree. Taking a closer look she found it was a grave containing the skeletons of three bodies, all female and they and been there for some years. A quick scan of the area showed no others. There was no marking anywhere to indicate their resting place so it was obvious there were not expected to be found. She turned back to the way they were placed. Not laid in any order, they seem to have been thrown in with no ceremony and hidden for good.

As Hashtag picked up the find he did a spiritual search of that area, going back slowly until he stopped about twenty five years before and then it all became clear. He immediately requested Bracket to do the same search for a grave in his area but just outside of the small town in the wooded area. As soon as he had the location he would home in and regress, putting himself in the position of the occupant of that time.

It didn't take long to locate a spot about two miles from the town and sure enough there were three female bodies all thrown into their grave in a haphazard fashion with no respect.

So now the two on this continent had a similarity and Marmaduke thought it best to fit the pieces together before trying to see the connection with the English one. The women had all been reported missing but never found so the families had lived with the awful knowledge that something terrible had happened and they would never know what.

It wasn't long before Marmaduke had everything placed in chronological order and it fitted perfectly.

Everyone was tuned in for the summary although they had the capability to still monitor whatever job they were already on. Marmaduke was only imparting thoughts in a split second but the information was in detail.

"Let us go back about twenty five years. The three females found in the natural grave at Niagara were all raped and killed by a young priest. Now we are looking at a single middle aged female that has been apparently raped by a passing preacher."

"But she wasn't." Hashtag offered.

"On the contrary, he was raped by her and it won't stop there."

"I thought he was back, doing it again." Bonnet stated.

"Probably what everyone would think." Hashtag added.

"For some reason she is taking revenge for what happened to her mother, who yes, was one of the three." Marmaduke explained. "And anyone would wonder how she would know, after all her mother was killed."

"Unless," Ampersand was getting the picture "her mother is working through her."

"So will she kill him?" Hashtag wanted to know.

"Just a minute. It hasn't ended yet." Ampersand was coming in from all angles. "Either she is going to do that, or she will go for as many other religious men as she can."

"There's something else." Bracket was keen to add.

"I was wondering when you'd get to that." Marmaduke had let them turn it over for a while. "If three were killed, why has only one come back for revenge?"

"The other two don't know how?" Hashtag guessed.

There was silence then they all came to the same conclusion. This was only the start. Anything could happen.

It was time to summarise the Pennsylvania case. This time the passing priest, a female with the Angels of Song had become entangled with a local bachelor who thought that when the group left he would go with them. That was fine, he would for a while and of course nobody would miss him, but she had no intention of making it a permanent arrangement. He would soon be history and revenge would be achieved.

"But this is slightly different." Marmaduke stated. "She is looking for two more men to take into her fold."

"Not alone." Hashtag was quick to state.

"You think she will co-opt two more from the choir." Bonnet was on the mark.

"I do. And I think it will turn out they are relatives of the other two women. Not necessarily daughters, but those who seek revenge."

"That means it's growing. They won't just take one man, but one for each woman." Bonnet mused.

Marmaduke let their thoughts run on but then addressed Hashtag.

"You quite rightly thought that the other two victims may not be able to get back to see 'justice' done or that it could be other relatives. Well consider this. There may be no living relatives but the victims may home in on receptors, two innocent members of the Angels of Song, and work through them.

This gave them all plenty to weight up and consider and in conclusion Hashtag reminded them of one important fact. The priest at Niagara twenty five years ago was the same one who killed the ladies in Pennsylvania twenty or so years ago.

This was going to be a situation that needed closely monitoring because, although The Paws could pre-empt many things, there was always the element of surprise and they had to be prepared for anything.

Sunset had been observing everything and voiced "You haven't included the English situation. Are the three ladies there involved?"

Before there could be a reply Hashtag cut in "Or the vicar?"

"In that case," Marmaduke brought them to order "there needs to be a similar scan near the villages for another grave."

As the conference finished, all were playing the facts through their spiritual thoughts in order to be prepared for whatever move would be made next.

Mary and her fellow worker Olive had to do the church flowers on Friday this week as there was to be a wedding on the Saturday. As she was owed some time she took the afternoon off work and picked up the blooms on her way home. Olive didn't go out to work as such but just did some local cleaning jobs to bring in a few extra pounds. Simon had offered to give Mary a hand but she knew that tongues would be wagging overtime as it was so didn't want to give them any extra fuel.

Rain was threatening and both ladies were glad to get into the building in case it poured down.

"Hope it's alright for the wedding." Olive said as they gather the various things they needed.

"Forecast isn't too bad." Mary smiled and spread out a cover before separating the flowers.

They had been working for a while exchanging the usual small talk but there was a sense of expectancy in air and both knew why.

"I wonder who the next one will be." Olive couldn't contain it any longer.

"Could be some time." Mary cut it dead. "The young ones seem to be going abroad these days or they get married in all sorts of places. The church seems to be the last on the list. Anyway it's nice to be having one now isn't it?"

"And of course," Olive had to add " most of 'em don't even bother."

"To get married you mean. well yes, there is that I suppose."

"Course it was unheard of at one time but now everyone seems to accept it." Olive knew she was laying a trap.

"Well, I for one certainly don't….."

Whatever Mary was about to say was cut short.

"Oh so you won't be running off to Ibiza or some such place then?" She'd got her on the run.

"What do you mean?"

Although she might not always seem the brightest star in the sky, Mary guessed she was being poked and wasn't going to give her the satisfaction of running straight round to the shop to spread what she, emphasising the 'she' had found out.

"Well, I mean, it goes without saying don't it."

"Would you mind passing me that carnation please, I just need one more for this."

Standing back Mary said "I think that's alright for the font, now what's left?"

Not liking to be ignored because she wasn't getting the news she wanted Olive pushed it a bit further.

"You're going to have a busy weekend then."

"Oh? Am I?"

"Well, there's the wedding tomorrow, I expect you've been invited to the reception, then Sunday services. You'll be needing a rest, you been looking a bit overwhelmed lately."

"Oh? I wasn't aware of it."

Olive eyed her up and down with a very knowing look and smiled.

"Make sure you don't overdo it that's all I'm saying."

As she made her way home Mary wondered why anyone should think she was overdoing it but then the thought of what she and Simon could be doing brought a flush to her face, among other places. If Daphne had been there she would have filled her in as to what was being suggested, adding it was a wonder the woman hadn't told her she was putting on weight.

She had no sooner walked in home and put her things down when the phone rang and it was Simon, no surprise there.

"How did it go? Did you survive the third degree?"

"Oh, alright. Um, you mean did Olive ask me anything?" The conversation had already gone to the back of her mind. "I hope you will like what we did. I thought it looked really nice."

There was a slight pause then he said "That display with the carnations in the white urn, was it supposed to be on the floor?"

"No, I put it on the font." She was surprised.

"Thought so."

"What are you saying."

"Leave it to me, I'll see you later." Then added "Love you."

"Love you too."

She put the phone on the table and everything was churning through her mind. She was sure she had put the flowers where she said but could she have been distracted?

Simon knew. He had seen Olive wait for Mary to be out of sight then double back into the church, and when she had left to go charging round to spread her gossip, true or false, he checked the church. Not only was the urn on the floor and almost hidden but other arrangements had obviously been moved. So the knives were out were they? Well he may be a peacemaker but he was no fool and they had taken on the wrong man.

The usual three were in conference in the shop and Olive had got the other two with their mouths open.

"Well, she gets out of breath that quick and don't ask me how many times she had to sit down, and had at least three pees that I know of."

"No, she isn't."

"I'm telling you she is. And she's put on a few pounds."

"No. Get away."

"Well her mind's not on what she's doing, made a right mess of those flowers I can tell you. I had to go back when she'd gone and redo most of them. Well those she'd done, mine were perfect of course. But you couldn't leave them like it, I mean what would people of thought. Might have said I'd done it."

"Thank goodness you did Olive."

"Makes you wonder how long it can go on."

"Aah. Truth will out, truth will out."

"Well I shall have to keep my eye on her." Olive stated to which the other two nodded in agreement.

They chewed the fat over any other slanderous bits they could muster and were so engrossed that they all jumped a mile when Simon entered the shop.

"A word Olive if you please. Outside." His face was like thunder.

"Well, I don't know I'm sure." She was about to demand that whatever he had to say he could say it in front of witnesses but then remembered all that she had been pouring out since she arrived.

He made sure they were in full view of the shop and surrounding houses but only she could hear his words.

"I know what you did." His accusation came out like a knife.

At first her guilty conscience let her assume he knew of her scandal mongering, then she remembered the flowers.

"What do you mean vicar?"

"I saw you go back into the church but you didn't close the door."

"I'd forgotten something, my scissors." She looked flushed.

He stared at her with a look she had never seen before.

"Would you have lied so readily had you still been in the house of God?"

She was trembling now but still he stared into her soul. Giving a little smile he said quietly "You don't look well, I would go home if I were you and sit quietly. Meditating might help. But you are very flushed, had any heart trouble?"

"Well a bit of high blood pressure now you come to mention it."

He put one arm across his chest, rested the other on it and cupped his chin with his hand.

"Tut, tut. You must be careful. No sudden excitement. Now can I walk you back?"

"No, no I'll be fine, thank you vicar." Then as if he was waiting for a reply. "I'm going now, just say ta ta to my friends."

He watched her pop her head into the shop and after a few exchanges came back out. and made her way home. Any onlooker would have seen a very caring clergyman offering comfort to a lady.

When she had gone he entered the shop.

"Good afternoon ladies. I hope you are both well."

"What's up with Olive?" The owner asked.

"Well it isn't my place to say but maybe she wasn't feeling too well."

He bought some milk and left leaving them wondering what was going on, because something was for sure.

Chapter 6

Either Elsie's death had made June realise what a mug she had been over the years, or she had been lying low waiting for the right moment to strike. The Paws were monitoring Wizard, who although appeared to be pretty innocuous, seemed to have a deeper spiritual connection to something or someone and it didn't take them long to work it out. But they were not alone. Elsie had her own suspicions for many years.

June had always had a cat since she had been married and although she insisted she took in the strays who needed a home, it was always dark grey or totally black. At one time she had frequented a spiritualist church she said, which her family laughed off as a passing fancy but it was in fact an amateur witchcraft group. Sadly some of these people have no idea what they are doing and what starts out as a bit of fun can soon turn into something sinister when evil tags onto them for their own amusement.

Elsie had noticed more about June that her daughter realised and firmly believed that the cats she kept were her familiars, supernatural entities that support witches. Although this was her own daughter she felt she was right, but how could she warn her against such practices. There had been occasions when something or someone had crossed June and then something nasty had happened to them in return. But her daughter had gone about in her quiet way, even being bullied but appearing to do nothing about it, so everyone thought. But this provided the answer.

The Paws traced back over the past fifteen to twenty years and the list of casualties was much more than they expected yet June was never suspected.

Wizard sat alone apparently unaware of anything around him for while The Paws could monitor from afar, other entities would be obvious to him but he didn't always respond to their presence. He didn't have to be on a high plane, his purpose was to support June who was also fairly low on the spiritual scale. But what was very useful was that he acted like a cctv. His observations were recorded in his memory and could be picked off at any time. He was the perfect camera.

The air had been electric since her visit to Daphne and Wiz knew what this meant. Someone was in for a shock. In this and the neighbouring villages the main topic for gossip was about the vicar and his new love. A few people passed on their condolences regarding her mother's passing but afterwards just got on with their own lives and problems and gave her little thought so the lack of visitors suited her perfectly. She knew she had Daphne and Ken worried which was just what she wanted and with each passing hour her determination grew to ensure justice would be done in some way or another.

She sat in her chair and Wiz knew he had to be close by so he took his favourite position on the end of the table, his attention fixed on her. Her hands had dropped into her lap and her head was resting against the back of the chair. She was totally relaxed. The cat's eyes never left her and he was completely motionless. After a moment of letting her mind drift she felt herself being lifted straight up at speed and for a moment she was confused for this was a strange place. There seemed to be women around her all trying to communicate at once and she felt the vibration of all their voices merging and getting louder and louder.

"Help us. Help us." Was all she could hear and then they seemed to be clawing at her and she felt the pain of their fingernails scratching at her arms. The last thing she remembered was some of them trying to drag her away as if they wanted her to see something.

"Oh!" She jumped as she found herself back in her chair with Wizard patting at her arm. "Was that you trying get me to come back?"

He merely looked at her for a moment then returned to his table end.

All this had meant nothing to June but The Paws had their answer. As they monitored her mental trip, they instantly knew where the third grave was and guessed she had encountered not only the souls of the six women abroad but the three buried locally, for they were certain there would be three, and many more who had met the same fate and were clamouring for justice and the truth to be revealed.

She was somewhat disappointed for she had hoped to get assistance in dealing with her sister. However it didn't dampen her determination to get her own back but she did need help of some sort and from any source. Not realising it, she was putting out an advert for any takers. Dangerous thing to do. The Paws put a protective wall around her, but knew that if she was determined to go her own way it would have to be pretty strong and that in turn could keep everything out, even good helpers.

Acting on this new information, Marmaduke was able to go straight to the site of the grave. With most of the villages being a couple of miles apart there were many little hidden places just off the connecting roads where anything could be buried and stay for a long time undisturbed. It seemed the fashion in the area to have little groups of trees at intervals so people out for a drive could stop in the shade for a break and take in the views. It was fairly hilly and made for a picturesque landscape and along the ridges of some there were a line of trees which had been planted as a windbreak. The tree groups couldn't have even been described as a copse they were that small but added to the charm.

It was one of these that had drawn the attention of The Paws but on examination there appeared to be no grave. Bonnet suddenly noticed something. She was concentrating on a patch of ground just outside the bunch of trees.

"I think this was bigger, there were more trees here and they have been cut down."

"You're right." Marmaduke wanted to be in on this one to see if the information they had harvested proved correct.

It didn't take them long to see the same pattern of three female remains lying in an untidy mess in their resting place.

"How long have they been here?" Bonnet wanted to know.

"Make a guess."

"Well it was possibly before the Niagara or after the Penna." Bonnet was musing.

"If they are all tied." Marmaduke stated then added. "Done by the same man."

Bonnet was using her special skills doing a rescan.

"I would say no more than about twelve years ago." She was confused because something wasn't right.

"Quite recent which is strange." Marmaduke was on the same wavelength.

In villages of this size if even one person went missing it would be headline news all over the area. So how could three go and there be no report of it because they did an instant check and came up blank.

"The only explanation I can see is that they were killed elsewhere and dumped here." Bonnet thought this must be it.

But Marmaduke threw another thought into the mix.

"Possible, but not all from the same place."

"Oh my." This was a new aspect on it. "But in a way it doesn't tie them all together, or does it? Would he change his M.O? Not usually."

Marmaduke let her go through all the options and stated "That is something I think we are going to find out."

Sunset, although still monitoring the residential homes to make sure they didn't slip back into the old ways, found her attention drawn to Elsie, not so much by her actions but the growing evil forces surrounding her. She called for an immediate 'cleansing' in the hopes that this tormented mother could find the peace she needed and progress at her required speed.

Cleansing could be instantaneous, or a battle depending on the power of the evil in presence. The lower playful yet annoying entities were no problem but sometimes a more powerful one would attach itself to an unstable soul, not for the purpose of causing them trouble but to use them as a temporary cover for their own practices. Bearing in mind the history which was coming to light, Sunset was on the alert for anything that may have been drawn into the area, for whatever purpose.

Elsie was flitting between her daughters and angry at their apparent callousness. It seemed so sad that, just when The Paws thought she had agreed to float away with her beloved, she would double back, yet again this wasn't unusual and they were prepared for it.

Now she was in June's house. Wizard picked her presence up immediately and he knew she wasn't alone although Elsie and the entity appeared to be attached as though she had trodden on something nasty and it was trailing along on her shoe. This was not good. Wiz wasn't sure whether to stay and watch or seek a safer place until it had gone. In the end curiosity got the better of him and he moved to his favourite place on the end of the table. What appeared to be a quiet room on the physical plane was anything but on the spiritual.

Elsie was venting all her wrath on June.

"I knew you were messing with things you didn't understand. Well now look where it's got you." She was inches from her nose yet June seemed quite unmoved apart from a sneer which was taking over her face.

"Where's the lovely caring little girl I brought up? Eh? Answer me that."

At that point her anger took over and she tried to swipe her daughter across the face but it had no effect in any way.

The evil that had followed Elsie now took an interest in June and planted vicious revenge in her mind building up the most horrible hatred towards her sister that hopefully would end up in death.

Wizard's attention had never moved from this presence and didn't trust it although he wasn't sure just what it was.

After several more rants and attempts at making her presence felt, Elsie left to rent her anger on her other greedy girl. Wizard noticed that as soon as the pair had gone, June's husband was with her almost begging her to get rid of the hatred and concentrate on him, but it fell on deaf ears on any level.

Elsie's husband was trying to stop her going any further with this but something made him pull back and observe closely what was happening. In horror he realised her hardly recognised her. Sunset had shown him through her vision what his once loving young wife had become. She was ugly and unstoppable. He was urged to leave now and hopefully he would have his true wife returned, but there was a lot to do before that could take place. Reluctantly, he accepted the suggestion and a guardian helped him from the area.

It was evening when Elsie timed her visit to Daphne and Ken, oh yes she wanted them both to experience just how much she despised the pair of them. He was a poor simpleton who needed a good kick up the arse, as she put it, and as for her daughter, there were no words to describe the contempt that was boiling up there.

"If only I'd been able to do this before." She imparted to her current guardian.

There was no answer for the sentinel knew this was not the time for common sense, reason or explanation and he was there simply to watch over her. Any intervention would come from higher up the ladder.

The couple had eaten their meal and settled down in front of the television.

"I've been looking forward to this." Ken said as he tossed his newspaper on the floor, realised the error of his ways and quickly picked it up and put it on the table.

"Hmm." Was all that came from the other chair.

"What the hell is……..?" Ken shouted.

"You must have done something with those damn controls. You're always playing with them."

"I haven't touched them. Look." He pointed to them on the coffee table.

"Hmm."

The screen was jumping and the picture started to roll. Next a piercing noise came from the speakers which was so intense they both covered their ears.

"Turn it off. Turn it off." Daphne was trying to yell but the noise was so bad it drowned her words.

If that was intolerable, what happened next left them speechless and trembling. The noise stopped, the screen went blank except for one thing. Words were appearing and getting clearer and bigger until they filled the whole screen. Both jumped back as the message seemed to come out in 3D.

'*YOU TWO FILTHLY ROBBING BASTARDS.*'

Then it was gone. Stunned silence filled the whole house. Ken sat motionless, his mouth open and a very damp feeling in his underpants.

Daphne was the first to utter very quietly "What was that?"

There was no reply for Ken had gone deathly white and passed out. She tried to get up from her chair but something was holding her back. In vain she tried to call to him but her mouth appeared to be gagged and she felt very sick. As quickly as it came it went leaving two very dejected people in shock. Something drew Daphne's attention to the screen which now displayed the words '*THIS WAS JUST A TASTE OF WHAT IS TO COME*'.

As Ken started to come round, the television resumed its normal broadcast. He looked at the set, then at his wife who was the colour of beetroot.

"I think I passed out." His words were hardly audible.

"Something happened." Was all that came as a reply.

"Oh." He realised he was wet but hardly dare say for he knew the reaction it would get but for once he was wrong.

"You passed out Ken, do you feel up to going and having a swill and changing your trousers?"

He was amazed but grateful for this unexpected turn.

"In a second. I feel a bit shaky." Then looking at her full on said "How about you? Got a bit of a colour, you have."

She was nearly in tears.

"Ken. Something happened here. I don't know what, but if it does it again, I will go crazy."

He looked across the room.

"Wasn't the telly playing up?"

"That's only part of it."

She didn't know how to tell him what had appeared. He'd swear she was going off her trolley so she passed it off with some remark about interference in the area but it seemed to be alright now. He appeared to accept that and slowly got up and made his way to the bathroom.

She sat there her heart pounding, everything racing through her mind.

"June, it had to be June." She decided. "I don't know what but she's had something to do with this. Her and her meddling with the funny business."

She waited until Ken came back down and they tried to keep their attention on the programme but somehow neither could concentrate.

"I'll make a cuppa when the adverts come on." She said, quietly for her.

He just nodded and felt very strange but couldn't describe it. The scene finished and just as the ads were due the screen went blank apart from a vivid red background and the words *'THERE WILL BE BLOOD'*.

Daphne leaned over, grabbed the remote and switched the set off. They tried to explain to each other that it must be something the tv people were trying out or even advertising another programme. Yes that was it!

It had to be something simple.

"Suit you two nicely then wouldn't it?" Elsie was triumphing as she left, but she would be back.

The Paws had a new lead on the grave near the villages. The reason the women had not been missed or even reported missing was because they weren't local. Hashtag had come up with the idea that they were some kind of travellers possibly gypsies or a circus troupe but then he found that they were actually evangelists who went round the country spreading the word through singing. This immediately made them all pay attention. Was this the connection with the current Pennsylvania Angels of Song?

Marmaduke weighed up the possibility that a group or family emigrated to Canada just before three women were raped by a priest or preacher man and then killed. Then five years after that in America three more met the same fate. Then did the same murderer then come to England and repeat the crime? But the first two still seemed to have little or no other connection with the English one.

"But even the first two aren't the same." Bonnet stated. "In America the females are looking for men we think, to do whatever they have planned but in Canada the, and I quote 'passing preacher man' raped a spinster. So that isn't following a pattern."

Marmaduke paused before delivering his next statement.

"But she wasn't raped. Oh they had sex but it was the other way round. She went for him and must be looking for......"

"Two more." Was the chorus.

Hashtag couldn't resist adding "An eye for an eye, only its three men preferably vicars in each case, just to balance the books."

"Ok so we have a situation developing which needs our attention." Marmaduke spoke. "We have to try and thwart their plans before any more innocent men are killed."

"And if we can't, nobody can." Bracket announced.

"Right. Ampersand will you stay with the Canadians and Bracket you follow the Angels of Song. Hashtag keep making your comparisons. Bonnet and Sunset you have a tough job."

They all knew what was coming next.

"You have to find out what is going on in England. There has to be a similarity somewhere as all these three started simultaneously as though someone had fired a starting pistol. It may all look innocent but we know it can't be."

Marmaduke knew from experience this was not going to be easy but people's souls were at stake and it was up to The Paws to save them from an existence of eternal damnation.

The weather looked promising for the wedding and Simon had purposely checked the church in the morning although the ceremony wasn't until 2pm. He had a strong feeling of distrust about Olive since the previous incident and he didn't mind if she knew it.

Mary was very excited almost as if it was her own wedding day and she had reason to be. She'd been out and bought a new outfit, quite a change from her previous attire, had her hair and nails done and paid special attention to her make up. Today she wanted to look stunning. When she had asked the sisters if they were coming to the service because everyone usually did, they were both extremely hesitant which was a surprise. There weren't many events, usually a small concert or a sale for which ever season it was, so anything like a wedding, or even a funeral drew them out of their doors. But Mary didn't care if they came or not except for one thing.

"If they don't come, they won't see my new look, among other things." She smirked for a moment then realised that with their Mum having just died and the funeral to arrange they probably didn't feel like it. She'd have had a shock if she had known the things that were brewing around them and June may not have felt it a good idea to enter the church with things that were in her mind.

It had come as quite a shock to Simon to learn that they weren't having a church funeral but going straight to the crematorium at the nearby town. He had prayed for guidance and even answers but nothing seemed to be helping him.

He was in his vestry just doing a last minute check of his vestments when he heard a slight noise coming from the nave.

He quietly opened door into the chancel and peeping round and saw someone leaving by the main door on the side of the building. Quickly he went down the length of the small building looking everywhere but all seemed in order. His long legs soon took him to the main door and he went outside scanning the little churchyard. Although he saw no one he noticed the gate leading to the village green swinging slightly so he headed off in that direction. Whoever it was had made their escape just in time for him to be able to get a proper look but he was sure it was a woman.

He went back into the church and prayed for the safety of everyone due to attend today and while his head was bowed, his hands together and his eyes closed he felt a warm sensation encompassing his whole being as the love and protection of his many guardians provided him with extra care.

It was nearly dinner time and Olive had purposely made her way to the village shop. Irene the owner always shut at one o'clock on Saturdays as there wasn't much trade after that and everyone knew that if they needed milk or any other necessary item they had to get it before she closed. Her other friend Pam was already there and the two seemed to have their heads together over something because they both shut up as soon as the door opened.

"Only me." Olive assured them.

"Put the closed sign on." Irene pointed to the door. "Nobody's coming in now and there's only a couple of minutes to go."

Olive did as she was asked as she couldn't wait to learn the latest gossip knowing full well something was afoot.

"I'll just put the cash in the safe, then we'll go in the back. Pam would you be a dear and put kettle on for us." It wasn't so much a request but they all seemed anxious to get their heads together.

A few minutes later they were all sitting round the small dining table drinking tea and eating some scones which were almost out of date. Olive decided to come right out with it.

"So what were you two on about then?"

The other two looked at each other then back to her. Much to Olive's disappointment the latest gossip had nothing to do with Mary or the vicar.

"That's it?" Her mouth stayed open. "I thought you were going to spill about… well you know."

"Well I do my best I'm sure." Irene seemed put out.

"Perhaps I can put my pen'oth in then."

They both looked at Pam.

"You knew something and you didn't tell me?" Irene almost shouted.

"Well, I guessed we'd all be here having a chin wag before the wedding and I wanted to save it." Was the excuse but it was obvious Irene was still a bit off.

"Get on with it then." Olive was just as eager to know whatever it was but it better be good.

Although there was no one else about Pam beckoned them to lean nearer while she whispered.

"You know my friend that works at the hairdressers in town, well, guess who went in to have her hair all restyled, and her nails done too."

She sat back with a smirk on her face.

After a moment Olive asked "You don't mean….?"

"I do."

Irene was still agitated. "Well who?"

They both looked at her as though she ought to have been the first to grasp it.

"Her of course." Pat looked pleased with herself. She had got a first.

There was a pause and Olive explained "Mary."

"No!" Irene sat back.

"I told you something's going on didn't I? Didn't I say?"

They both chorused "Yes you did say." Just to shut her up but she was still crowing.

"I knew it." Olive brought her fist down on the table. "She and him have been invited to the reception."

The others looked at each other and then back at her.

"You don't get it, whether they are or not, she's not done it for that." Irene tried to explain.

"Well why else would she get all dolled up?"

"Right," Pam stood up, "times getting on and if we're going to get a good seat we'd best be doing ourselves up a bit."

Olive rose but added "You're wrong if you think it's just for him."

"Why is that?" Pam felt a bit deflated.

With a disapproving snort Olive picked up her bag and said over her shoulder as she left "He's not looking at her hair or her nails while he's stoking the fire is he?"

"She's got one thing on her mind she has." Pam tutted.

"Truth will out." Irene had hoped for something a bit juicier, but was prepared to sit back and watch.

Although it was still summer, anyone could be forgiven for being confused, for one day could be beautiful and the next pouring with rain and cold. So it was the luck of the draw if anyone planned an event and they had to prepare for all eventualities. Simon was pleased for the wedding party that today was mild and promised to be dry so everything should go smoothly. His mind was constantly on his new love and he couldn't wait to see her as she had told him she had bought a new dress and hoped he'd like it. He was fantasising that it was their wedding and he knew that wouldn't be too far off for they had promised themselves to each other. It hadn't been officially announced but by the time the service was over everyone would know, for the gossip would spread round the church in seconds.

If excitement was brewing in the village, it was nothing to what was going on at high levels. The Paws had several options and although some could be amended along the way depending upon events, there were some that, when once started could not change. In previous severe situations where innocent people were at risk, the drastic step of removing the individual or even whole group of evil entities had to be taken. In this case it would mean that they would have to wait until they were absolutely sure about the identity of those who were at present in body for false trails could be laid. To remove so many in order to take their souls for cleansing took precision and The Paws knew better than to go off half cocked. So homework had to be done, and quickly.

One of the main factors in the current situation was movement. It also tied into the fact that the English grave may hold such women. The Angels of Song were permanently on the move as was the preacher man in Niagara along with others yet to be claimed. While the past locations were known in all three, in the present situation to date there was only proof of the North American ones as the English village was yet to give up its secret of who was being targeted and the predators. Maybe it was time to cast the net a little wider. Marmaduke needed to know if the sisters were involved and why their mother seemed to be hanging around so told Bonnet to be extra vigilant. Although the victims seemed to be outsiders, nothing could be taken for granted.

She decided to keep her attention around the village during the wedding although Daphne and June wouldn't be attending but she could monitor many places at once so this was no challenge. Other guardians had been asked to try and remove Elsie as she was a distraction at the moment and Bonnet was keen to see the effect on the couple without her meddling. June was her own worst enemy and if not watched would be under the power of undesirable spirits as she was just about opening the door to them. Revenge is a strong emotion and if not harnessed becomes a killer in itself, gaining power which will only be used to achieve the user's goal, and they won't stop until it has been executed.

But Elsie too was on a mission and surprisingly enough very agile when it came to sidetracking her warders. Feeling rather sheepish they had to admit she had eluded them. Sunset was well aware of the talents of the guarding angels so if this being had outwitted even them, it meant she was of a much higher level than it had appeared. This could change the dynamics and the rest of The Paws were instantly aware of this.

With Bonnet keeping her attention on the villages, Sunset set off to investigate and was soon tracing Elsie's wake. Strangely enough it seemed to have hovered near the grave on the top road and then faded to nothing more than a faint trail no larger than a strand of cotton. This was immediately logged by all the cats and they realised this lovely old lady was not what she seemed.

Hashtag joined the communication pointing out that when she was born it was many years before the first attacks started ie twenty five years ago and surely this didn't date back that far. Marmaduke was quick to remind him that on passing over she could have been taken over and used. Evil can pick up on the tiniest emotion and she was very upset at the treatment of her girls and even more now she was learning the truth, so she would be a prime target.

"In that case," Hashtag was weighing up the possibility "she would still leave a wake unless…."

Marmaduke took over here. "……the power using her was strong enough to erase most of it for her."

But then the question arose. Why? If she was just being used as a tool for their purpose, it must be something pretty important.

"And they use her to mask their own identity." Sunset added.

Whatever the reason for now, it would be down to The Paws to trail her movements as any less angels, however high their level, could be identified. No, the evil must not be aware they were being tracked. That was of the utmost importance. Sunset would have to be on constant full alert for Elsie may not appear as previously but could be made to be whatever the evil intended. All Paws would not be able to relax for a second.

Chapter 7

The church was filling up quickly for the wedding. Several pews at the front were reserved for the wedding party and guests so the villagers were trying to get as near as they could in the seats available. Olive had earlier left something on one of the seats to look as though it was taken and the vicar, in his urge to find out who the person was, hadn't noticed it.

In a gap between everyone arriving, Mary very carefully timed her appearance. At first nobody took any notice and just assumed she was one of the guests, especially when she took a seat in one of the reserved pews. But there was something familiar about her.

"Who's that?" Irene whispered.

"Not sure, but I'm sure I've seen her somewhere." Pam was straining to look but the church was too full to get anything but a back view.

"Well, I'm surprised that one certain person hasn't come." Olive's lips were pursed.

The other two looked at her, then back in the direction of Mary.

"No. it can't be," Irene started to say out loud then changed it to a whisper.

Olive half stood to get a better view.

"Nah. Hair's wrong colour."

But as soon as the words had left her lips they all remembered what Pam had said and all three tried to look again.

"You didn't say she had it dyed." Irene hissed.

"I don't know. My friend said she'd had it styled."

Olive did the folded arms under the breasts move which she always did when she was going to make an announcement.

"Well, I'm going to find out." She stated firmly.

"Not now." The other two chorused.

"Of course not now, but as soon as they leave I'll be the first one to give her a going over. And," she gloated "if it is her, I was right."

They looked at her as much as to say "Why?"

Olive sighed. "I said I bet she'd be going to the reception. With him."

"Oh she did." Pam nodded.

If they were going to discuss it further, they were cut short by the organ announcing the arrival of the bride. While the rest of the congregation were looking at her and her dress, the three women had other things on their mind.

Bonnet had been watching the proceedings and knew she could return at the end of the service for nothing very interesting could happen until then, although she had a way of leaving an invisible alarm that would alert her just to be on the safe side.

Her main attention was still on the sisters and what struck her was the difference in them. She hovered over Daphne doing her shopping in the neighbouring town. Ken followed very unwillingly but knew he had better help with the bags and if she was in his sights, at least he knew what she was doing. She had seemed very unstable since the telly incident and was getting quite jumpy, always asking 'What was that?' or 'Did you see that?' It was making him on edge and he was getting sick of it. Bad enough that June had finally found out about the money, and he didn't know where that was going to lead but his dominant wife scurrying around as though the bogey man was after her was too much.

"What have you put them in the basket for? We don't eat those." He grabbed some ready meals and put them back on the shelf.

She stood there open mouthed for a moment then looked in the trolley back at the shelf and then at him.

He tutted and just asked "What else is on your list?" He'd had enough and wanted to get home.

How they got anything was an achievement but as they drove home he noticed she was getting more edgy.

"What's up with up with you?" He snapped.

"Nothing."

"Oh well that's alright then."

They drove in silence and he had never been more relieved than to pull into the driveway. He got out but Daphne stayed where she was, looking straight ahead.

"For Christ sake woman, are you going to get your arse out or sit there all day?"

He slammed his door and went to unlock the house. Ignoring her now, for she was really getting on his nerves, he unpacked the shopping and put the bags in the kitchen.

Going back to the car he opened her door and said "Well stay there for all I care. You're doing my head in." And strode back into the house.

He put the kettle on, although he felt he could do with something a bit stronger, and got two beakers out assuming she would come in when she was ready. He turned to get the milk and jumped for she was standing behind him.

"Good god woman, don't creep in like that."

He walked past her and went to lock the car. When he came back she had finished making the tea.

"Right," he said fairly calmly as they sat down in the lounge, having put the groceries away, "are you going to tell me what's eating you?"

She turned slowly and looked at him.

"There's something going on."

He merely nodded as if to ask what.

"You haven't noticed it have you, I can tell. Well it's freaking me out, good and proper."

He sipped his tea and asked as nicely as he could.

"Um, what is it that I should have noticed?"

She didn't speak for a moment then looked at the tv.

"That for a start. You blacked out, and then….then...the dreams."

"What dreams? You didn't say nothing about any dreams."

"Me Mum." She had gone quite pale and was on the point of tears.

"Alright, I can see it's got to you, but if it was only a dream, I mean you're bound to be upset, she's not long gone and she was your Mum."

"You don't understand. She knows."

It took him a minute to work out what she was trying to say.

"Hang on. You trying to tell me that she visited you in a dream and told you she knows what we did?"

She nodded and looked down at her lap.

"Well, that's just your imagination. How could she know? Think about it."

She shook her head vigorously.

"She knows I tell you and what's more….."

"Well?"

"She's going to haunt me for the rest of my days."

He'd heard enough.

"Claptrap. What a load of rubbish." He wanted to say bollocks but knew that wouldn't go down very well. "And you believe it."

"So would you if you'd seen her."

He snorted and carried on with his tea. She felt she had to explain so turned and looked straight at him.

"Listen to me. She came at me only she looked horrible. It was her alright but her face had changed and I've never seen such hate in anyone before. She accused me of everything and said I hadn't known the last of it as long as I existed, either here alive, or when I'm dead she will be there taunting me, reminding me of the upset I've caused, unless……"

"Well, unless what?" He wasn't sure he wanted to know but had to ask.

"I do as she tells me, then I will be forgiven."

He stared back at her.

"Listen up. You had a nightmare that was all. Your Mum wouldn't have done that. I'll tell you what it is, it's just your guilty conscience and the fact she's died, all together came out in a bad dream. I've heard of that before. She didn't visit you so get it out of your head."

Bonnet watched the little scene but knew Ken was wrong. Elsie, or what appeared to be her certainly had been in contact with Daphne but what she would be instructed to do to save her soul would not be of a pleasant nature for it must have come from an evil source as good spirits don't make bargains.

Although it may be difficult to understand, while this little scene was being played out, Bonnet was simultaneously monitoring June and it must be remembered that the information was being transferred to every other Paws member. Although there was really no need for them to meet to pass on anything new, they did hold conferences to decide upon the next course of action.

When this cat was weighing up various subjects' characters and habits, she would wave her virtual tail to and fro in a very hypnotic rhythm as though stirring the matter to find an answer. She was in this mode as she surveyed the difference in the two siblings. Daphne was obviously crumbling under the supernatural happenings and would soon crack whereas June seemed to be thriving on anything slightly out of the ordinary and was beginning to believe she was implementing it and was in total control.

At this moment the woman was sitting in her chair with Wizard on the table end and she was calling upon the spirits to help her make Daphne pay for her dishonesty and greed. But there was more to it. She rather liked this new feeling of power and was going to develop it to the greatest extent, then they would see who was calling the shots.

Although she had no idea quite what to say, she reached up her arms and started calling to anyone who could help which was a very dangerous thing to do for it was an invitation to any playful or very evil entity to use her for their own ends, not caring particularly what she wanted. Bonnet had immediately put a shield around her and drawn attention to lower level spirits to put a constant guard on to prevent her from going past the point of no return. But there were still those lurking around looking for any willing soul so diligence was essential at all times.

Whether or not June was going to get any outside assistance, the revenge brewing inside her was its own power source. As she sat alone now she mused on what would hit her sister most, and her husband for that matter for he didn't have to go along with everything she said. Then it hit her. When they had been small, Daphne use to taunt her behind the mother's back so that she always appeared to be the caring big sister, but she used to threaten June that if she said anything, she would regret it. It didn't have to be anything big, but the continual nudging or humming was mental torture.

Taking a deep breath, she reached for the phone and dialled their number. It took a long time for one of them to answer.

"Hello." It was Daph.

"You wanted me." June stated without emotion. "Well you rang me and put the phone down when I answered and I know it was you because your name came up on caller recognition. So, what did you want?"

"But I didn't, did I Ken? Ken." Daphne yelled to get his attention.

He looked up slowly. "Did you what?"

"I didn't ring our June did I?"

"Dunno." Was all he grunted.

"Well let me refresh your memory." June was being very snide now. "You have rung me at least three times today so you must have wanted something, unless…….."

"Unless what." Daphne was getting irate and snapped the words out.

"Well, let me see now. You could be loosing it altogether, or you could have reverted back to your childhood. You do remember your childhood don't you dear sister and all the games you used to play."

"But…" Daphne tried to cut into the flow.

June wasn't having any of it. This was more like it, she was top dog now.

"But of course you made sure Mummy never knew and do you remember the threats you used to make if I squealed on you. Now let me think." She was really milking it now. "Ah yes, you said you would cut my hair off, and put one of dad's cigarettes on my arm, alight of course."

"I don't have to listen to this rubbish." Daphne yelled and June noticed. a slight ring of hysteria.

"Oh but you do because you see I'm waiting for my first payment from you both or….you will be able to read all about yourselves in the local paper, followed by the national press."

"You wouldn't." Daphne turned to Ken. "She's threatening us."

"What with?"

"Oh I'll tell you in a minute." Feeling he was a waste of space she turned her attention back to the phone. "Now look here June, I don't know what your little game is but…" She stopped. "Hello. Hello."

But June had hung up.

Sunset was getting very concerned for Elsie's safety. This was the trouble when souls were not at peace when they passed and they needed extra care and supervision or they were prey to some of the most cruel entities who would use them and then discard them when they had no further need of them.

In this case, although Elsie's actual spirit was being safely guarded, an evil source had taken possession long enough to use her image for their own ends. If they could make the sisters believe it was really their mother that was visiting them, they had them in their power to carry out their own evil plans. Although the wake had been minute and could have been overlooked by lesser individuals, Sunset had other powers enabling her to trace Elsie. She didn't blame the guards for any negligence because they were constantly up against some very high powers and it was an eternal fight.

But Elsie, although going through the calming process was still not at ease. She had been terribly hurt by what her girls had done and found it impossible to rest. If any opportunity arose where she could possibly slip off on her own she would take it.

Bonnet was aware the marriage service had finished and was keen to see the reaction when the busy bodies left the church for she knew what game Mary was playing.

A lot of the congregation had gone out while the register was being signed in order to get the best position to take photos and throw rose petals, which were easier to clear than confetti.

Seeing this, Olive beckoned the other two to stay put as they would get a better view of Mary when she left. With the door being about half way down the aisle, it meant that everyone in the party had to parade in front of them so they had a grandstand view. The two pews in front of them were now almost empty so they quietly moved forward. Now they would see without a doubt.

The wedding march struck up as the newly weds and their immediate family emerged and were followed by the rest of the guests. Mary was walking alone at the back and had left a good yard gap so that everyone had a perfect view of her new look. Also she had removed her gloves and had her left hand resting on her right.

The nudges that went on between the three women must have caused bruises. Their whispers were so loud that if it hadn't been for the organ, everyone would have heard.

"Look at that!" Olive had to be the first.

"It is her, I thought so." Pam was nodding.

"Well, she scrubs up well I'll give her that." Irene was very approving.

"Yes but look, at her hand." Olive was getting frustrated with them.

"Oh. Oh." The other two chorused.

"She's engaged." Irene stood there, her mouth wide open.

"And she is announcing it to the world." Olive knew this meant that she couldn't be the first to go spreading it around the village. "Bit blatant if you ask me."

"You have to admit, she does look fancy. Just shows you doesn't it?" Pam was admiring her wishing she could look as good as that.

Olive had suffered enough of this admiration and cut in "Hadn't we better go out now?"

The others agreed and knew it would be an opportunity to get a closer look.

"Ladies." The vicar's voice broke into their thoughts. "I hope you liked the service."

"Oh we did vicar, and the flowers held up well didn't they?" Olive couldn't resist a little dig.

He held out his arm, beckoning them to precede him and to be polite they had no option although they were dying to ask him about Mary.

Bonnet surveyed the scene with some amusement but also shared her concerns about the engagement as none of The Paws were sure if this hadn't got something to do with the current revenge programme.

Marmaduke had come to a conclusion. Even if the families who emigrated had kept in touch in the past, the current ones had no connection and lived their lives to suit themselves. None of them had any leaning towards anything spiritual although a couple of them went to the local church on Sundays but apart from that were very down to earth folk. This meant that whatever was brewing was from a totally different source and the purpose was as yet unknown.

"Just when we thought we were getting somewhere." Hashtag wasn't one to give up and was annoyed at the setback. "But the similarity has to have some bearing." He mused.

Ampersand and Bracket were still having to be extra vigilant in their areas as this was the time when shields could drop and the evil would take over. Bonnet was still worried about the local vicar because her instinct told her something wasn't right but as yet she couldn't place it. Sunset was still overseeing the residential homes to make sure there was no backsliding, but there was the double problem with Elsie. The mother couldn't rest and was becoming more and more determined to teach her daughters a lesson, but there was also the question of which evil had taken her image, for what purpose and for how long. She hoped it might be one of those cases where her shell was being used and would be discarded in which case it shouldn't have any adverse effect upon her. But others would believe it had been her and that was the problem.

For now they must watch but there was another aspect. With The Paws unique talents, they could pre-empt, move into the past and observe things in the present which were not noticed by any other force. So whatever or how many were working this underlying plan must be somewhere near their own level and that was particularly worrying for the situation could change by the second, and all the homework might as well be thrown out of the window for everything could be a load of red herrings hiding what was really going on. This was a very serious conjecture but one which could not be ignored.

June still felt she had the power to control people but it needed to be nurtured although she didn't feel she wanted to seek outside help. She had considered going to one of the spiritualist churches but what she had in mind would have been shunned. She had to get back at her sister and her pathetic excuse for a husband in some way, some lasting way. Her own late husband was of no use as he only wanted to love her but she needed revenge and the seed was growing until it was becoming her main purpose. She glanced at Wizard.
"And as for you, you're no help. I thought you cats were supposed to be good at this sort of thing."
Although Bonnet had steered the necessary help in her direction, revenge is very powerful especially when sprinkled with a bit of hatred, for those two alone make a very potent cocktail. This woman was reaching desperation point when the idea came to her.
"I don't need to call on any help, I'm quite capable of doing this myself." She stated aloud as if to press the point. Rising to

her feet she said in slow very menacing tones "Get ready people, you don't know what is going to hit you."

She waited until evening just as the sun was going down and shadows were starting to form strange shapes, and drove to Daphne's house. Parking out of sight, she walked the rest of the way and wandered round to the back of the premises. It was obvious by the flickering they were watching television in the front part of the room and being a through lounge she had a perfect view from the back window.

"Fancy not drawing the curtains." She laughed as she sarcastically thanked them for being so considerate.

If she had a plan to annoy or frighten the pair, she may as well have forgotten it for at that moment she felt a tremendous force stream past her and start to rattle the windows. Whether or not it was having an effect upon the occupants was nothing to what the shock did to June. Instinctively she hid behind one of the large bushes, her heart pounding inside her chest and she felt very sick.

Ken appeared slowly at the window being very cautious.

"Can't see anything." He called over his shoulder. "Must have been a gust of wind."

"Well go outside and look." Daphne called. "Just to make sure."

"Why don't you go if you're so keen to know?" He sat down in his chair.

"You're the man."

"Oh well, thank you for that." The sarcasm dripped off every syllable.

"Well, are you going or not? Something must have caused it." She wasn't letting go but there was no way she would have ventured out.

Before either of them could say any more it happened again, followed by the lights flickering and a strange humming sound echoing all over the house.

That did it. Daphne covered her ears and started screaming "Stop it. Stop it I tell you."

Ken was at a complete loss. He wasn't scared but at the same time did feel rather uneasy.

"There's got to be a simple explanation." He decided but still didn't move from the room.

While the two inside were trying to fathom the spooky feeling, June was still behind the bush but trying to see what was going on. Suddenly she felt two icy cold hands on the back of her shoulders and she was literally marched away from the house and pushed against her car. Never had she driven home so quickly. Once inside the house she flopped down in her chair trying to understand what had happened. This had gone too far. It didn't work. Something was fighting her. She looked across at Wizard and wondered if she would be better resorting to legal ways because she seemed to be the one who was being controlled.

Wiz blinked and if cats smile, he smiled as he thought "That should trim their antics for a while."

Bonnet had to agree with him. June wasn't of any level to be playing with what she didn't understand or have control over, so to get her out in the early stages seemed the best. Now they just had to keep her out. It was sad to see the reaction of her sister and Ken, but in a way they were getting their comeuppance for now, but it had to be monitored and controlled or again the door would be open for any playful spirit to take advantage which in turn would attract more. But you never knew with people and some just seem to have a self destruct button ready and waiting to be pressed.

Elsie's guardians had been instructed to let her have a little rope but with a tight hold on it so that she didn't get into danger. The Paws were all curious to let her be at large to draw out whatever was using her image, for they knew that, as they had control over the real one, whoever was using the duplicate could then be traced. It seemed very doubtful that it would simply be a playful spirit due to the way Elsie's wake had faded.

Sunset was ready to monitor the moment she was released. It would be rather like opening a cage for a bird to fly when it was ready, as opposed to taking it out. She had to feel she was moving on her own and if she felt she had put one over on her guards, that was fine.

It didn't take long for her to seize the opportunity. When she thought the guardian wasn't being diligent she was off like a rocket. Sunset was monitoring her instantly and as usual the rest of The Paws were aware of what was going on. It was just past midnight and within seconds Elsie was hovering between the villages, almost as if she was uncertain as to which daughter to torment first.

But she was the bait, for Marmaduke and Hashtag were scanning the area waiting for the double to show itself.

"Perhaps it's already finished with it." Hashtag ventured.

"Possibly. But I don't think a higher power would bother with such small fry. No, it could be keeping it back for something special." Was Marmaduke's theory and the other cat had to agree.

Suddenly Elsie homed in on the vicarage housing Simon Hughes. She hovered over the empty building for a moment then slowly descended into the house checking each room as though she was looking for something in particular. When she reached the bedroom she went through every drawer, examined every item in the wardrobe and slid under the bed. Coming out on the other side her attention went to the bedside locker. The usual stuff was on the top and in the small drawer. Although it didn't make any difference to her, she did notice the little cupboard underneath was locked. Examining the contents, she drew back with a satisfied smirk. She had found what she was looking for.

Sunset passed the thought that this was very different to the restless mother who wanted revenge on her children and the question arose as to whether or not this was indeed the original Elsie or the doppelganger. This called for extra diligence and the guardian that had been instructed to release her was now told to watch the area very carefully for any signs of movement.

Elsie now left the vicarage and headed for Mary's house. This too was deserted and the process was repeated although there seemed to be nothing of interest here. Again she hovered as though planning her next move. Sunset watched as Elsie seemed to be taking stock of everything in the surrounding area then suddenly changed course and was at the group of trees on the top road near the grave. She certainly seemed to have a connection with this place in her spiritual form, but was there any significance to what may have happened here when she was in body?

During this sequence nothing had come to light regarding the duplicate form which could be anywhere by now, or being kept in hiding until needed. Unless, as Marmaduke reminded them, what they were monitoring now could in fact be the duplicate and Elsie's soul was being held elsewhere.

Chapter 8

Simon and his 'guest' had stayed at the wedding reception long enough to be polite but then he made his excuses before the disco started. Everyone understood that he had to take communion in the morning and thanked them for joining them.

As he drove Mary home he pointed out that it was the first time they had been alone all day. He had already said many times how beautiful she looked, but strangely enough something was niggling inside that he had fallen in love with the original Mary, and the lady beside him, attractive as she was seemed different. There was a more blasé attitude and a 'look how lovely I am' air about her which he found a bit unnerving.

"I know the witches saw my ring, I made sure of it." She bragged.

"Witches?" He was concentrating on negotiating the tight bends on this bit of road and didn't look at her.

"You know, the three at the church. Well I certainly gave them something to look at."

If he had previously imagined that she would be wearing it quietly with a slight blush in her face, how wrong he would have been. Also, to put it kindly, she didn't always quite understand what people were talking about until it was explained, but at times today she had been holding the conversation, almost to the point of boredom. Could a ring make that much difference?

He stopped the car near her house, got out and opened her door for her.

"You really should have some sort of light on this path." He said looking up and down the way to her house.

"Oh it's not far. And anyway, who would want to molest me?" The words came out in a purring tone.

They walked to the front door and she got out her key.

"I'll just see you in, then I must be off." He said quickly.

"What? You aren't coming in?" Her mouth was open in disbelief. "But I'm your fiancée. You don't leave a fiancee on the doorstep."

There was a small bulb that was part of the doorbell unit which shed a small amount of light on her face and as he looked at her in the gloom, for an instance he thought his eyes were playing tricks on him. She had changed into the most grotesque creature he could imagine, but it was so instantaneous he knew he must have imagined it.

He rubbed his eyes and said "I must drive back before I fall asleep."

"But darling, you can either leave the car here and walk or…..you can stay with me, after all it's almost legal now."

Something was pulling him away with such a force it didn't take much to resist and he ran back down the path leaving her furious for she had failed to bed him.

Bonnet had sensed that something was very wrong and had rescued Simon as soon as she could. The Paws had been monitoring the changes in people's characters knowing the various evil groups were to blame and these were causing a distraction to the main task in hand. Every time the cats seemed to get a lead on the USA, Canada and even the English situation, something always popped up and took their attention elsewhere. Although they were quite adept at multi-tasking, things of this nature required top concentration levels. It was as though some force was hampering them, so what was so important that mustn't be discovered? Of course other powers wouldn't know it was The Paws that were involved, they would merely think it was some high level angel power that must be stopped.

At this point The Paws executed one of their tricks. They carefully engineered that various decoy groups be put into operation, without their knowledge of who was behind it. The groups would think they themselves had come up with a brilliant scheme to flush out the current wave of evil that was sweeping various points on the globe. It could also have its advantages if any groups were disposed of, but Paws knew that the ones they were after wouldn't be caught by lower levels. But it would give them something to occupy them for now.

It was time for what The Paws referred to as 'The Wave'. As they were always on some mission, either separately or as a group, every so often they called a conference. For a millisecond in human terms, all cats would pause, sit in an upright position and their tails would wave simultaneously slowly from side to side. During this time all knowledge already fed into their computer like spirits, was sorted into categories with nothing being discarded. Even the simplest inoffensive piece of data was stored somewhere. This complete, they continued to pursue their immediate assignments.

Mary was somewhat dejected. She had put a lot of time and money into her new look and fully expected that, after the reception Simon wouldn't be able to keep his hands off her. It was almost as if he didn't like her and couldn't get away quick enough. Surely he hadn't gone off her. With these thoughts racing through her mind, she slowly took off her clothes and looked at herself in the mirror. She screamed in horror, for what was looking back at her was something hideous and it was laughing. She wanted to turn away but something was holding her head still. She closed her eyes, but they were forced open and held. In utter disbelief she was looking at the image that had scared Simon away although she didn't know that. It was beckoning to her now. In panic she realised this wasn't human but some sort of beast, almost a mixture of several things but the mouth was opening showing huge teeth dripping with slime and it was coming for her.

Suddenly there was a crash as the mirror shattered and the hold upon her had gone. She slumped to the floor sobbing and shaking uncontrollably. How long she was there she couldn't tell, but as she opened her eyes she began to think she had just experienced a bad dream. But she wasn't in bed so had she gone to sleep on the floor? Realising she was naked she automatically reached for a gown to cover herself. As she pulled it on it caught on her ring and she clutched at it with the other hand crying "What have I done?" She looked for the broken glass but the mirror was in tact. After a few moments of telling herself she had to do it, she walked to the mirror and looked at herself. The only reflection was her own. There was a peaceful calm in the room and Mary felt as though loving arms were protecting her. She moved to the phone to ring Simon, but stopped.

"He'll think I've had too much to drink. That I'm trying to get him to come back." She mused and put the phone back down.

"I'll ring him in the morning." She decided but was feeling rather apprehensive for the way he left her still lay heavy on her heart.

Sunset had teamed up with Bonnet the moment she knew Simon had to be removed and had stayed with Mary knowing she would need help. As the evil tried to take over the poor woman, Sunset struck and the entity never knew what hit it. The illusion of the mirror was simply to pull Mary away but what went on out of sight was only for The Paws to know. Enough to say the thing wouldn't be coming back, ever.

The two cats knew they had disposed of this evil doer, but that was only one, although word would have spread immediately and other less powers would take heed. The problem was always that higher powers would take this as a challenge so the guard must always be up.

Marmaduke was sharing his thoughts.

"Was this just a playful sprite having its bit of fun, or a warning?"

Hashtag had been homing in on this and had his own thoughts.

"It was drawing too much attention to itself, and keeping us busy."

"A decoy." Was Marmaduke's first answer.

Bonnet had been watching Simon since he had been home.

"I'm not so sure. Could be a route to the vicar."

No one needed to ask why, the fact of the religious connection had to come in sometime.

"Someone is using Mary to get to him. She isn't doing it, she is just a tool." Hashtag thought it was a possibility.

Marmaduke said "I was wondering when he would enter into the plot. There had to be a vicar, preacher, or whatever in the English sector and he has been sailing under the radar up to now. Wonder if it's going to become clear."

"About time." Hashtag stated. "Whatever is being planned, it's well under wraps."

"We can only do what we're doing." Sunset reminded him. "If we jump in ahead, it could all be ruined."

This was something they all knew and had no choice but to adhere to, besides there was so much more to unearth before the finale.

When Sunday morning dawned Daphne was on edge. She knew June was up to something but if she confronted her with it, her sister would come the innocent 'Can't think what you mean' routine. At least with it being the weekend she knew she couldn't be taking any legal action, but what might she be doing on Monday?

"Stop fussing about it." Ken kept telling her.

"It's alright for you to say. She was right on one thing. It can be proved."

"What?"

"With the bank entries of course."

"Oh."

"It's not just that. I can probably talk my way round it and say she was in agreement. Now, there's no proof of that is there?"

"So that's alright then."

Daphne sighed. He couldn't see or he had a short memory.

"No, listen to me." She tapped him on the knee. "You must remember when she starts playing around with her voodoo stuff. Well look what happens."

If she thought that was enough to enlighten him, she should have known better.

"She starts with those weejee boards and stuff." She never could say it correctly.

"Oh that." Ken sniffed. "Well as long as you don't start meddling in it."

Frustration came out in a snort.

"Oh listen to me will you. I don't get involved but she starts, well, thinking she has powers that she hasn't that's all."

""Well, that's alright then isn't it. If she only thinks she has, can't do much damage just thinking."

"Am I the only one in this house that can see the danger?" She was almost shouting now. "It doesn't have to be her. She could attract the wrong sort."

He looked at her, stood up and said very slowly and precisely "Why don't you go and see the doc on Monday. Can probably give you something."

"What?" She spat out.

As he turned at the door he said with some force "To stop your brain going crackers and imagining there's little green men going to pop out and wave their tackle at you."

With that he slammed the door behind him and left her open mouthed, partly from shock at his outburst and upset that he could never take her seriously. Well he would see, and then who would be doing the shouting?

The Paws were doing all they could to keep June safe from interlopers but as they had already agreed, there were some who would never learn. When June woke up, the memory of the previous experience was fresh in her mind, but she started to believe that she had controlled it and it was she who had actually sent it packing.

"Now, if I can do that, what else can I muster?" Were her thoughts as she lay in bed.

Bonnet was doing her best to wipe her mind but if someone insists on hanging onto anything, they can become obsessive and it takes priority. June would not be satisfied until she had locked her sister in a funny farm, as she liked to put it.

"What do I need with extra help?" She mused. "I'm quite capable of pulling this off on my own, but a little extra fun along the way won't go amiss."

Pulling on a gown she went downstairs to make a cup of tea but jumped as she approached the landing.

"Oh Christ, you made me jump. What the hell are you doing there?" Her outburst flowed out quite naturally.

Wizard sat staring at her barring her path.

"Get out of the way you stupid animal or you'll be down those stairs with my toe up your bottom."

Still he held her gaze.

"Oh well you asked for it." She yelled and her foot came out to kick him. "What?" As she looked down he was at the bottom of the stairs staring up at her, but she had made no contact with him.

"Hmm, must have had a rocket up his bum."

She went down stairs carefully in case the creature decided to leg her over. Then she stopped.

"How did you get through a closed door? I left you on the table in the lounge."

He continued to fix her with his gaze and after a moment it began to unnerve her so she quickly opened the door. He simply turned to the front door.

"Oh you want to go out."

She unlocked the door and watched him go slowly past. Pity she couldn't see his face which had the distinct expression "Stupid cow."

Having made her tea, she sat in her usual armchair letting her mind decide her next move. After a few moments she had it, and no one would ever suspect what she had done. How could they? She would simply be the caring sister who only wanted the best for her sibling, added to which, of course, she was grieving terribly over her late mother. And if Daphne's mind wasn't right, it could be believed she had tried to rob her own flesh and blood without knowing what she was doing. Yes that was the plan. Put her away where she belonged.

Hashtag was bewildered, which wasn't like him. There seemed to be no movement at either of the North American sites. It was as though everything had come to a standstill. The spinster at Niagara didn't seem to be seeking out any more vicars to seduce, while none of the Angels Of Song had been dragged under the priestess's wing to assist her in acquiring two more males. It was as though nothing had ever happened.

Both Ampersand and Bracket had been using their powers to calm the situation but it never happened this easily.

He suggested re-examining the graves at both to see if he could spot something previously overlooked. Although it suggested something had been missed, The Paws were quite used to going over things time and time again, so none of them was offended at such a practice.

First he went to Niagara and let his spirit float into the past as he descended into the soil. For a while he adjusted to the surroundings but then he noticed a strange smell. At first he couldn't place it, but then slowly he was aware of what it was and what it was used for. He readjusted to the present and visited the Pennsylvania grave. Again he went through the same ritual and again there it was, the smell was the same. It was chloroform, so all these ladies had been rendered unconscious before they were possibly abused and murdered. Quickly he requested the English grave be examined in the same way and Sunset was immediately on to it. But she came back with the news it was not affected. Without wishing to be rude, Hashtag asked if she would mind if he too gave it the once over to which she readily agreed.

All The Paws waited for his findings. Sunset had been right, there was no smell of chloroform, but he had detected the tiniest trace of another odour.

Sunset was also keeping a watch on Elsie, or what was acting as her for she obviously had a connection with the English grave. At present she was constantly on the move almost as if she was trying to hide her trail. It was noticed that she hadn't bothered with her girls which was surprising as they were the reason for her unrest. This gave The Paws all the more cause to think she had been replaced, but that gave added concern as to her whereabouts.

Mary hadn't gone to communion and knew that Simon would want to know why. Sure enough as soon as the service was over he was knocking at her door.

"Are you alright?" He asked as he strode in. "I wondered where you were."

As he spoke he was getting flashbacks of the creature he had seen last night.

"I...I.. think so." She said softly.

"Were you too tired, only you didn't have a lot to drink and I wondered…" He didn't know quite what he wondered or what to say.

"I'm alright, really." Her voice cracked but as soon as he took her in his arms she broke down and blurted out what had happened in her bedroom.

"Oh thank God." He murmured to himself for now he knew it wasn't her or another side to her, it was an imposter, some evil that had temporarily taken over her being.

"Look, I want you to see a friend of mine." He said gently.

"You don't believe me, you think I'm mad." She cried.

"No. No. Quite the contrary. I think something got to you and I want to make sure you are rid of it."

She held back. "You mean I'm possessed."

He drew her back to him. "No but I think you were the victim of a passing evil and I want to make sure it doesn't happen again."

She looked a little relieved. "Of course, you know about these things."

He paused. "Mary, there are certain ones who do this all the time, rid people of unwelcome visitors. Fortunately I don't come across many such cases and when I do, I call in someone who has had plenty of experience. Do you understand?"

"Yes. I think so." She looked far away for a moment. "But why me?"

He didn't want to worry her further so answered "It doesn't always have to be anybody in particular, just someone they use for their own purpose, then they move on and annoy somebody else."

Her mouth was open. "I think I know what you're saying."

He smiled and kissed her gently.

She was still trying to work it out because the old Mary had returned and it would take a moment to sink in..

"So if they did what they did, won't they have gone anyway, I mean do I have to see somebody as well?"

"I just want to be sure." Simon smiled. "Leave it with me for now."

As matins was at the next village today, they arranged that he would pick her up after breakfast to go together, then with evensong being at this village he could keep a watchful eye on her, also she would be in holy places which all added to the protection.

Bonnet was pleased at the outcome but she and Sunset would still be on the alert in case all was not as innocent as it seemed.

It must be pointed out that, although the entire Paws group were working on the current problem and possible evil threat, they were all carrying out other jobs simultaneously, such was their talent. It was nothing for any of them to be monitoring several serious situations around the globe and keep abreast of all of them. Sadly there isn't room to cover the extent of their work, that is, all that we can imagine for most of it is known only to them.

The three cronies, were going to matins in Irene's car. They didn't always go to every service, sometimes choosing between the morning and evening which ever was in their village, but they wanted to keep up with everything that was going on, especially where Mary was concerned. Olive and Pam met at the shop and soon the car was full of continual speculation.

"I wonder what time she got home." Olive started the flow.

"Ah. But who's home?" Pam laughed.

"Perhaps he stayed with her." Irene offered.

"Nah." Olive was on the ball. "His car wasn't there all night, I'd have seen it. He'd never get it down that path."

"I wonder when they'll publish the banns." Pam was thinking it was all so romantic.

"Well they'd better hurry up. She won't be able to carry a sprog soon." Olive said with some force.

Pam's mouth dropped open.

"But she must be past it by now anyway. Well just about." Irene put a different view on it.

"How do you know they want any? Maybe they just need each other."

There was silence for a moment then in chorus the other two chimed "No. She'll want his offspring."

"I wouldn't be too sure on that." Irene looked smug.

"You know something." Pam called from the back seat.

"Me? No. Just looking at the facts."

They drove in silence, all deep in thought until they arrived at the church.

With all the little villages being within a mile or so of each other it was quite usual to see the same faces not only at the churches but at any event that was being held. The ladies nodded to those they recognised but were eager to see if Mary had surfaced and what she looked like today.

"Bet she's got bags under her eyes."

"He might be as bad."

This was followed by a stifled giggle.

"Don't think much of these flowers." Olive was casting a critical look around. "Must have picked them out the hedgerow."

"There she is." Irene nudged them.

"Where?" Pam was straining to look.

"Not up there. Level with us. Look, no don't look now."

"Well make up your mind." Pam hissed.

"I don't believe it!" Olive had spotted her. "What's happened?"

"Well, don't go and ask her. I know you."

There was a slight titter. "My word, she's lucky to have come out alive."

"Will you two stop it!" Irene felt as though everyone was looking at them. "Calm down. You can talk to her later, nicely."

"As if you aren't bursting to know." Olive couldn't resist pointing out the truth.

How long this would have gone on none of them could have guessed for then the organ struck up and the service had started.

Marmaduke was pondering over the smells in the graves. The two in North America had a vestige of chloroform which had been thought to have played some significant part in the deaths, but maybe that wasn't the case. Was it possible the smell had lingered on the murderer's clothing meaning he could have worked in a hospital, or were the females all nurses or even doctors?

He now compared this with the English grave. The smell there was so faint it would have gone unnoticed on normal examination but Hashtag had regressed and picked it up from twelve years before. It was embalming fluid.

This had to mean there was some connection after all. The murderer must have worked in a hospital or an undertakers and had killed three women on each occasion. The question then arose, had he killed them all at the same time or separately, kept the first two bodies until he'd added the third and then buried them altogether.

Hashtag queried if it mattered apart from the fact that there was definitely a modus operandi in all other respects. At first the cause of death had been touched on but when Hashtag examined the bodies as they had been when they were buried, he confirmed they had all been recently raped, strangled and also badly bruised but not stabbed in any way.

"Just wondered if he didn't like blood," Marmaduke thought "but that would cancel out him working in a hospital or mortuary. He wouldn't have to be squeamish."

"Could be just the way he worked." Hashtag mused. "Depends on what his motive was." His tail was waving in a distinct manner.

"Go on, you're on to something." Marmaduke knew him only too well.

"Just going to recheck something." The air was still for he had already gone.

"Why is it that when you want somebody to do something, they don't do it?"

Sunset was wondering why Elsie, having led them a little dance to the vicarage and Mary's, seemed to have gone to ground. Maybe she was satisfied in what she had found and decided to be at peace, but that couldn't be. She appeared to have ignored her daughters and why did she visit the site of the grave? It seemed a distinct possibility that she was in fact the double so that meant they had to find the real Elsie.

As Hashtag had recently revisited the grave she asked him if he could throw any light on Elsie's wake as she was aware how faint it had gone. That had to be when they did the switch. It was imperative to find out who had taken her and where, as the poor soul would be in torment.

Bonnet cut into the thoughts. "What do we do with the double?"

"Try and hang on to her?" Was Sunset's first reaction but then said "Unless she is a plant. While we have her she can find out all about what we are doing."

"Except she can't." Hashtag reminded her. "Oh she can observe on her level, but nobody knows what we do."

She felt a bit put out. "I am aware of that. I was using the 'we' as the good angels."

"I know." He corrected not wanting to upset her and sent a warm vibe to her.

"I am concerned about her." Sunset continued. "I don't think she is of much use to them, and I feel she will be returned when this character has completed her task."

"But we want her to progress at what should be her normal pace." Hashtag agreed then added "Come with me, it will only take a blink."

"It's ok." Bonnet offered. "I'll keep a look out, the ladies aren't doing much at the moment and I can soon home in closer if they get lively."

Before any human could have blinked Sunset had returned and Hashtag had resumed his enquiries across the pond. Bonnet had picked up on the scan and was waiting for her friend.

"Well, that was unexpected." She greeted her.

"It's one thing observing from afar, but when you really get in close contact it is very revealing." Sunset seemed very surprised.

"There seemed to be more than one or even two, am I right?"

Sunset paused. "There were three."

"I can understand that. Elsie, her double and the evil conducting the switch." Bonnet knew something was wrong as she said it.

"There were three Elsies. As the evil came in, she split, all the trails faded and only one of them came back."

There was a moment as it all sunk in.

"Elsie has been three entities all along, not just since she passed." Bonnet was trying to get it absolutely right. "And her soul had to go to the grave and…" She hesitated.

"Maybe it wasn't an evil force that took her." Sunset finished it for her. "She had been concealing a triple identity while in body which had to split upon her passing."

They both absorbed the facts as did the rest of The Paws. Ampersand seemed certain that there was a definite connection with the grave and wondered if Elsie's three spirits could be the three women on the top road.

"But she was born long before they were murdered." Bonnet thought.

Marmaduke cut in. "She could have been used when they were killed to help bring the truth to light. So she would have used one soul since birth, then twelve years ago, either carried the three as well as her own, or the three took over." He paused. "I don't think she was ousted or she wouldn't have been so concerned about her girls."

"I hate to be pedantic," Sunset almost apologised "but then, wouldn't there have been four when her wake nearly disappeared?"

"Good point." Marmaduke agreed. "But put it all together, when you thought she had split into three, her own soul could have been taken at that point leaving the three to return, in which case she is, as you thought, being held for the time being."

Bonnet's thought hit Sunset. "Ever wished you hadn't asked?"

"We all got that." Was the chorus from the rest of the group. But the moment of humour didn't diminish the seriousness of the matter. Now Elsie, or whoever she was had to be watched closely, and hopefully the real one traced.

Chapter 9

Having just finished their Sunday lunch, Ken sat back in his armchair and switched on the television while Daphne washed up. She was still a bit nervous about having it on in case of a repetition of the other night, but she had to admit it hadn't happened again and so hopefully it would never do it again. Ken had said that sometimes the channels test things and it could well have been that. She was just coming back into the lounge when the front door bell rang.

"Who's that?" She asked.

"How the hell should I know?" Ken wasn't too pleased at being disturbed and just wanted a peaceful afternoon with no silly business as he called it.

"I'd better go and see who it is." Daphne said as she slowly went down the hall.

"It's the only way you're going to find out." He muttered under his breath.

As she opened the door, Daphne gave a quick gasp of surprise. "June."

Without being invited June walked straight in almost knocking her sister out of the way.

"Hello Daphne, I thought I'd just pop round to see if you're alright." As she walked in the lounge she greeted Ken and asked how he was.

"Alright." He said abruptly and turned the sound up on the tv.

"Ken." Daphne hissed. "Turn it down, we shan't be able to hear ourselves think."

"Why don't you sit…" before she could say down, June had already parked herself in one of the easy chairs.

The air was somewhat tense but June seemed oblivious to it. She didn't wait for them to ask why she had come but carried on talking as though she hadn't a care in the world.

"Now, I know we haven't exactly seen eye to eye recently but I think we can put it all down to the sadness of Mum, God rest her soul, passing."

She looked from one to the other. Ken wasn't listening, or gave a very good impression of it, whereas Daphne was eyeing her up very suspiciously.

"I think you made it perfectly clear." Her sister said very firmly.

"People always say things they don't mean, and if we can't get on now, when can we?" June beamed but the smile was false.

"June, why have you come? Because if you've got something up your sleeve, you'd best come out with it and have done with it."

"Oh my dear, you mustn't get excited, we don't want you having one of your turns do we?"

"Patronising git." Ken thought.

"One of my turns? What are you talking about?" Daphne was getting angry.

"Now you see, that's what you mustn't do, get all wound up over the slightest thing. It's not good at our age you know."

Turning to Ken she asked "Does she take her medication regularly?"

Daphne blew now. "Excuse me lady. I am in the room. If you want to know anything you ask me."

June leaned forward. "Not been seeing things have you?"

"What do you mean, seeing things, what are you getting at?"

Daphne felt that somehow June knew about the messages that had been plastered across the screen. The reply was slow in coming accompanied by the fixed sickly smile.

"Well, it wouldn't be the first time would it, I mean think of those nightmares you had when you were little. Now let me think, things were chasing you if I remember and you were afraid to set foot out of the house and Mum had to drag you to school."

She turned to Ken again "Oh it was so funny. Everybody laughed at her."

He completely ignored her, pretending she wasn't there and hoped she would go.

Facing Daphne again she came in with her ace shot.

"Now you're not to worry." She lowered her voice and leaned forward. "It's obvious you aren't well, and that's only to be expected, but I can arrange for you to see someone."

"What are you drivelling on about?" Daphne was on her feet. "I know your little game, now take your stupid ideas and get out."

June rose to her feet, picked up her bag and said "Yes, the signs are well and truly there I'm afraid." Then to Ken "You must be blind if you can't see it, but you are heading for trouble by ignoring it."

That got a response for he too was on his feet.

"Now you listen to me woman. I want you out of this house now and you are never to set foot in here again. Do you hear me?"

"Oh loud and clear. But don't worry, I've seen enough to know where she should be."

He felt on the point of hitting her but suddenly remembered Daphne saying about the messages on the telly and a doubt crept into his mind.

"Just get out." He said.

"I'm going. Oh yes and by the way, you'll both be hearing from my solicitor shortly and of course the courts. Bye."

Still with the fixed sarcastic smile on her face she walked out of the door giving a little wave over her shoulder as she went.

Daphne was in the chair sobbing when Ken returned from shutting the door.

"Don't let her get to you. It won't help."

"She's trying to say I'm going crazy, and do you know what? I feel as though I am."

Although he tried to comfort her, he didn't know what to say or what to expect in the coming days.

The Paws were used to coincidences which often turned out to be either planned happenings or spiritual intervention so when the attention concerning the English grave coincided with news from Pennsylvania they were on full alert. Remembering that it was believed the English women may have been evangelists who spread the word of God through hymns, Bracket was now relaying that The Angels of Song in Pennsylvania were on the move. It was as though a signal had been given. The priestess suddenly had co-opted two more 'sisters' and these three would go off away from the group and seemed to go into some sort of trance. The priestess still had her male follower in tow, but there seemed to be no more men involved.

As he communicated, Bracket alerted The Paws that this time they had taken the man with them and they stood in a clearing in a small wood, almost on top of the grave. He was in the centre with his eyes covered in a cloth and the 'sisters' were surrounding him holding hands so that he was trapped. As Bracket watched, his insight was shared by every member of the group. Hashtag did a scan of this lone male and came up with the fact that he had been a lay preacher at a chapel but had been asked to leave, a fact he had never divulged. But the sisters knew and that's who they had been looking for. They had been in no rush for it was as though all the cogs had to move at the same time, so what had pushed their button?

The concern now was that Bracket knew why the priestess had no intention of taking him when they moved on. He would not be alive. What they were witnessing could be his last moments and this may be the first in a trio of revenge rituals.

The usual problem had to be addressed. If The Paws intervened too soon, they may lose valuable information about future plans, but if left too late, a possibly innocent young man could meet an untimely death. If it was indeed a revenge killing it would be unjust and had to be stopped.

Instantaneously they asked Ampersand if there was any action at Niagara. The spinster was still in the neighbourhood but there had been no action since her interaction with the passing preacher and she hadn't been looking for any more as they expected. Marmaduke wasted no time in doing a trail on the man and came back with some interesting information. He had passed to spirit soon after his visit to the town.

"She killed him then, just after they had, or rather she had seduced him?" Ampersand wanted to know.

"Sadly, he killed himself. It seems he had been told to by some divine power."

"So she didn't do it." Ampersand was feeling ashamed she hadn't found this out.

Marmaduke picked up on her thoughts.

"When he left, we thought he had just moved on and our attention was on her next possible victims. But yes, she did do it in a way. You see she had a different way of working. Acting alone, she worked on his mind and it was she who ordered him to kill himself. Not the angels or God or any good power. She had already taken her revenge and carried on in the midst of the town folk letting them think she was the victim of rape."

"Well that gets rid of one theory." Hashtag announced. "They are not all working to a wake up call."

"Like I said," Marmaduke repeated, "she had her own rules and acted in her own way. Very clever to get the job done before anyone was on to the plot."

"Do we do anything with her?" Ampersand was feeling a bit redundant now.

"I think you should still watch her. We don't quite know what we're up against and she could be biding her time. Let us not assume." Marmaduke stated to the agreement of the rest of the cats.

Before they took the English grave into account, the obvious job was to decide what to do about this poor chap in the wood, but that was about to be arranged for them.

Apart from Mary's hair, the rest of her had returned to her normal look. She felt she had lived through a nightmare and if it hadn't been for the fact she was wearing her ring, could have thought she had imagined it all. What had come over her? She lay in bed knowing she would have to go to work and face the barrage of questions about the wedding, Simon and anything else the women in the shop fired at her. As she worked in a small town a few miles away, at least they would only know what she told them as none of them would know any of her neighbours, or so she hoped. Her phone rang.

"Hello my lovely lady. How are you?" The tone was soft and loving and immediately she felt better.

"Simon. I am alright thank you. Just thinking about getting up."

"Good. Can we meet when you come home? How about coming here for your dinner?"

"Oh now that's something I can't refuse. Can we have your favourite?

"You can have anything you like."

She smiled to herself. "I think I can face the day now."

"Good. I've got a few jobs to attend to but won't be too busy. After all I haven't got a funeral to arrange."

"I know. Everyone is saying how disrespectful. I mean she was their mother. Doesn't seem right."

"Well," he sighed "people must do what they think best, and anyway there is a wedding to arrange." Then for a tease he said "Unless you want it in a registry office."

"Simon, you beast." She laughed and he was glad to hear she seemed to have recovered from the incident unscathed.

It took them another five minutes at least to say goodbye as they blew kisses to each other and didn't want to be the first to put the phone down.

Bonnet watched with some amusement resisting the temptation to imagine the fact that, had she been in physical form, she would have been glad they had hung up or she would have been sick!

Sunset was on the alert as 'Elsie' seemed to be on the move again. Each time she did they all hoped they would come up with the answer regarding the grave but those on the American side were also alert in case of a trigger reaction. Something in their senses told them that things were coming together but maybe not in the way they expected.

As Elsie drifted away from her holding zone, Sunset was monitoring from afar but noticed an extra determination in the mother's manner. Whereas she had previously been looking for something, she was now on a purpose and headed straight for the top road. She positioned herself over the grave and hovered for a moment her arms outstretched as though beckoning for something to come near. The air shook slightly as if being disturbed then two figures emerged, only as a mist at first but gradually they took the form of adult females although their faces were very indistinct. The Paws were all fixed on the image as the three joined hands and stood in the same position as the Pennsylvania trio, but this time there was no man in the middle. The air was changing now. From the gentle morning breeze it became heavy, stagnant and gloomy and the atmosphere was one of absolute hatred. The three figures were slightly off the ground then suddenly without warning descending into the earth and were gone.

Sunset wanted to follow but the others warned her off. Hashtag did a projection into the earth and saw that the three had become one heaving mass covering the bones of the three victims.

The questions now were this. Were these the souls of the three women, or relatives still seeking justice? Neither could be disregarded at this stage for nothing was obvious apart from the fact that the three must be using Elsie as a cover for their own use. That in turn left no clue as to where Elsie was.

"But why the attention to the grave, it's as though they know we are watching and want us to investigate." Bonnet thought.

"Without knowing we exist." Sunset added. "But they want attention brought to it so that the truth will come out."

Bracket reminded them that unlike his case, these hadn't got a victim but Marmaduke quickly added "Not yet."

Hashtag had been thinking.

"So spinster in Niagara has already disposed of her preacher man, or been instrumental in him taking his own life. The song birds in my area have got a previous preacher to kill for retribution but….." He left the rest for them to weigh up.

Bonnet voiced it. "These haven't found one yet."

"Or they have but haven't run him to ground." Sunset suggested.

"The only likely one is the vicar." Bonnet suggested.

"But he's not a preacher man." Bracket corrected. Different religion, more stable not nomadic like the others.

The picture was forming that this was not a haphazard selection but a certain type of man was needed and although there seemed to be a religious connection running through it, they kept hitting stumbling blocks.

Marmaduke had a theory. "We keep thinking that these are the spirits of the departed, or relatives, seeking revenge on men especially preachers etc. But what if they are also looking for relatives of the murderer or murderers."

There was silence for a moment. They were pretty sure the two North American incidents had been perpetrated by the same man, Hashtag was sure of that. But the English one wasn't. Yet there had to be a connection in some way for them all to be activating together. This had to be solved.

Without warning, Elsie and her attendants emerged from the ground and at that point The Paws knew by instinct that they had not opened their thoughts far enough, for this crime scene was different in one distinctive way and it was so basic all the cats felt ashamed they hadn't addressed it before.

Olive couldn't wait to pop into the shop on her way to her little job.

"Oh my, you should have seen her. I'm telling you, I can't work it out."

Irene was used to her gabbling on but there was no sense coming out of the woman and she wanted to know the latest more than anyone.

"Get on with it. What's happened?" She almost snapped.

"Well you know her hair?"

"Yes."

"It's the same!"

Irene was on the point of strangling her any minute.

"Well I would imagine it is. What's so special about it?" Olive smirked.

"That's just it, that's all that's the same as she was at the wedding. But oh you should see her now, looks as though she's been attacked or something."

Irene stopped what she was doing.

"Wait a minute. Just what are you telling me?"

Olive took a deep breath.

"I'm saying that after what we saw at the church, and we all saw her I might add," a little sniff for effect popped out, "but this morning she's back to how she was. Apart from her hair as I just said."

"Well that's mighty odd I must say." Irene was trying to fathom it out. "Hang on you said she looked as though….."

"She's been attacked, yes, that's just how she looks."

There was a pause then they looked at each other and said in unison "He's done it."

They stood there motionless for a moment then Olive said "We ought to tell Pam but I've got to be off." This was much to her dismay as she knew that as soon as she stepped outside the door, Irene would be on the phone, not only to Pam but half the village. But she had no choice and left making up her mind that she would let people know who had been the first with the news.

She hadn't been gone long before the shop door bell went.

"Oh good morning vicar." Irene beamed. "Lovely wedding wasn't it?"

"Indeed it was." He returned the smile as she handed him his morning paper.

"I must say how lovely Mary looked, scrubs up really well doesn't she?" Her eyes were on him for the slightest indication of unease.

"Well yes, but I like her as she is, for what she is."

"And of course you're engaged now." Irene was prodding.

131

"We certainly are. I'm a very lucky man."

This wasn't going anywhere so Irene stepped up the pace.

"You both had a busy weekend, must be tiring." She still watched for any telltale signs but none came.

"Well, it's my job and it does have some very pleasant moments but you work many hours doing a service to the community as well. A very valuable one I might add." Picking up his paper he smiled and left the shop knowing full well she hadn't got what she was looking for.

He had guessed Olive would have her telescopic eyes everywhere and would notice Mary might be showing the signs of her recent unpleasant encounter, also that she had tried to return her appearance to normal, so he had been ready for the inevitable third degree.

As he walked back to the vicarage his mind turned to Elsie and the fact he would not have the chance to conduct her funeral. Her daughters didn't even want him to go to the crematorium and had hired a celebrant to do the necessary. Although like many others, the family was spread through the local villages, everyone knew everyone. The little hamlets in total didn't cover as much ground as one of the large towns. Even when there was a vicar per village they all attended the various events and when they were reduced in numbers, the local one was almost covering everything. It could be expected not to have a church service with some of the younger people, but to those that had been brought up locally it was unheard of.

He made up his mind that he would pray for her soul at the time of the committal, it was all he could do.

The Angels had stripped their prey and with the help of a hallucinating drug had him in their power and were about to administer their final act. As Bracket was sure he was about to witness the horrible death of this young man, he was aware of a new visitor in the wood. But there wasn't just one. In a complete circle they advanced, chanting quietly until they had the women and their prey completely enclosed. It was hard even for him to describe them but all The Paws had seen this before. The spirits gave the impression of people covered in some sort of hooded robes although there was nothing solid, everything was like a heavy mist and floated in until it was one complete mass with no escape.

All The Paws were now aware of what was happening and had to stay back and let the lesser angels carry out their task. There would be death, but not as planned. The mist split so that part of it surrounded the man protecting him completely while the rest smothered the three songsters and removed them to a place further into the wood. With their powers, the man was helped to dress and guided to a place where he would be found with the knowledge placed in his brain that he had been attacked. There was even a head injury as though he had been struck and all traces of the drug removed. They left him in a dazed condition and that would be all he would remember, the ritual having been deleted from his mind.

This group of vigilantes were not to be messed with for they stepped in to a situation and justice was done, in their way. Although it was frowned upon by higher levels, it had to be admitted that only the evil was attacked and the good rescued. As quickly as they appeared they had gone leaving the three female bodies hanging in the wood to be found in due course. It would be assumed that one of their rituals had gone terribly wrong.

"I hope nobody thinks we did it." Bracket thought.

"Unlikely." Marmaduke assured him. "This group are known, they work alone and some of their ways are, well rather offbeat to say the least. Whereas our methods, although not so dramatic are long lasting and effective, plus we don't exist."

"Well that's certainly put a new light on things." Ampersand was still feeling a little redundant but still keeping watch on the spinster just in case whereas Bracket's allocation seemed to have been closed.

"Strange that it finished with only one man in each case." Hashtag was musing again.

"It may not have been planned that way," Marmaduke stated, after all the angels were rather interrupted. They may have had others in their sights, we may never know."

"Well mine's doing nothing, not even looking." Ampersand added.

"Which brings us back to England." Sunset and Bonnet had the feeling something was about to blow both physically and spiritually.

It was decided that Bracket would still keep a surveillance on Pennsylvania for now and Ampersand would continue to watch Niagara as one couldn't be too sure and none of the cats wanted to be caught out.

"Well I don't know what to do. She'll have to come with us in the mourner's car."

Daphne was going over the arrangements for the funeral on Thursday. As usual Ken was letting her take charge because that was the only way to be. He'd learned that over the years.

"Are you going to tell her?" His eyes never left the television.

"I suppose I shall have to but I don't want to ring her and I don't want her coming here again."

"And remember," Ken reminded her "you said you were never going to set foot in her place again."

She looked at him. "I don't suppose….."

"Oh no. I'm not asking her. You're making the arrangements." He crossed his legs as if that was the end of it.

"Well, I shall wait and see what she does. She's bound to want to know."

They were both quiet for a time while Daphne tried to decide what to put on the card going on the flowers.

"Are we having food?" Ken asked again without turning his head.

"When?"

"After the funeral."

"I've told you, why don't you ever listen? The undertakers are putting on a small tea back at their place."

"How many for?" He was interested now.

"Only close relatives."

"How many?" He was insistent.

"Oh, eight or ten. Our kids are coming of course but I haven't heard if June's lad is. You never know with him."

"Well we're not paying for someone who may not be there."

"That's another thing." Daphne hardly dare broach the subject.

"What now?" He dreaded to think.

"She should be coughing up for this not just us."

He looked at her now in disbelief.

"Are you completely off your trolley? She's not only expecting all this to come out of your Mum's money, but she's going to drag the pair of us through court because we've stolen most of it."

"What are we going to do?" She looked dashed.

"At this rate we'll be taking out a loan."

There was complete silence until the phone range and they both jumped.

"Who's that?" Daphne looked at Ken.

"How the hell should I know?"

"I don't want to answer it."

Knowing someone had to he got up and went to the phone.

"Hello."

There was a short pause as he put his hand over the receiver and mouthed "June."

Daphne did a gesture as if to say she was out but Ken shook his head and seemed to be pointing frantically at the phone.

"What? No I can't I will be at work. No because I'm already taking time off on Thursday."

He looked at Daphne whose head was going from one side to the other.

"Look its best if I wait for the wife to come back and I ask her. Yes I'll ring back." He slammed the phone down.

"Well?"

"She says she has arranged an appointment with the solicitor for Wednesday afternoon and we are both to be there."

"Bloody cheek." Daphne exploded.

"Well I told her I can't but...." He looked thoughtful.

"What?"

"I'm not sure what her game is but I'm not going along with it. Then we'll see just what she's playing at."

"I don't follow." Daphne looked completely bewildered.

He sat down and thought for a moment.

"Ok." He decided. "Correct me if I'm wrong but didn't she say we would be hearing from her solicitor?"

Daphne knew straight away. "Yes, it was almost her parting shot yesterday."

"Well, I thought they sent out letters telling you what you'd have to do."

"And what it was about." She added.

"Quite. So why would we be asked to a meeting, after all we haven't been accused of anything have we?"

"Do you know Ken, you're right. I don't think there is an appointment, and especially the day before the funeral."

They both looked at each other.

"Right lady," Daphne was feeling better "so you want to play your little games do you?"

Ken had to smile.

"Now what have you got up your sleeve?"

"Try to make me out to be loopy would she? Well two can play at that one. Then we will see who needs locking away."

"You're trying to get us off the hook." Ken fell in.

"That as well for good measure."

She looked back at the table where her notes for Thursday were spread about.

"And as far as I'm concerned she can walk, because she's not riding with us."

Chapter 10

Something had been niggling at Hashtag since his last visit to the English grave and to verify his suspicions he went again.

"Well?" the others wanted to know.

"Just got to regress again to be sure but something has been well hidden here."

Marmaduke now also wanted to clear up a point. He had weighed up everything that had happened before and recently and said that if they could put some of the facts to one side they could concentrate on what was still unsolved. He wanted to just concentrate on the North America venues for now.

He agreed with them all that there had been some sort of revenge plan in place but it hadn't gone as expected. In each case three spirits had been sent to co-opt three women in body and take out three men preferably vicars or preacher men, call them what you like in retaliation for the murders twenty five and twenty years ago.

He addressed Ampersand.

"Yours was the biggest failure. They picked the wrong one in the spinster who went her own way instead of following orders and her sick mind drove the man to kill himself. Of course she could not be found guilty of his murder as she hadn't done anything physically, apart from have the sex she'd been missing all those years. She made no attempt to get two more to join her and basically that's were it ended."

"Good in one way." Ampersand thought.

Then he turned to Bracket.

"At least the angels who stepped in saved the poor blighter and although he'll bear the scars mentally, at least is still alive and no more men will be used."

"More a success." Bracket said then thought "But not for the planners."

"No, after all their scheming, only one man died."

"Will they try again when a few years have passed?" Bonnet wondered.

"They may very well have an attempt." Marmaduke answered "but they know some force will be ready so they will have to change their tactics."

They all knew his summing up was right, but that left the English grave.

"I think we had better leave that until Hashtag has all his facts together." Marmaduke declared but added "Continue to keep a close watch on those you've been tailing. But Ampersand you join Sunset watching Elsie in case there is a split. There are still three remember. Bonnet you cover Mary and the sisters and Bracket you now watch the vicar. Hashtag get on with your investigations and I will keep my eye on the three gossips, not that they seem important at this stage but it also leaves me to join any of you who might need back up."

As they left, Hashtag passed them a parting shot. "And yes we were all right, the murderer near the villages was female."

As usual all this had taken place in the blink of an eye but at least they felt they could concentrate on what was going on in England because that was the biggest enigma. It was also a wise move with what they were about to learn.

Simon wanted Mary to marry him as soon as they could arrange it so that he could be with her as much as possible. He sensed something unholy was hovering and she needed his protection. Also at their age there didn't seem any point in waiting. Since her fright she had returned to her simple way of looking at things, not always getting the point straight away which he found sort of endearing. It was very unlikely they would have a family and he didn't like to pry into the personal facts too deeply knowing he would find out sooner or later. But it didn't matter as long as he had her.

She had never imagined love would come along now. Of course she'd had many crushes in her younger years but somehow the lads didn't fancy the old fashioned side of her and liked the more willing girls which was evident by some of the rushed marriages. But there will always be those certain females who, having got the one they want aren't going to let them go and use whatever means available to keep them.

The question of who would marry the happy couple was obvious. With two vicars sharing about four villages, it would be the other one. They didn't want an elaborate do, just something simple and then a couple of days away so that he could be back for the following week's services. She would move into the vicarage so her little home would have to be sold but that wasn't pressing and they would have plenty of time to sort it out without rushing things.

That would give the three cronies something else to chew over although there didn't seem much they could add to what they had already nosed into. But you know gossips!

Hashtag soon had his answers and he knew that from now on they would have to act with caution. Every move would have to be planned to minute precision or it could all go horribly wrong for some people.

The Paws were on full alert.

"It seems" he started "that our beloved sisters also had a younger one but the girl had always felt she should have been a boy. Now that may not seem unusual but in this case it was the attitude towards her that was her enemy."

He let that sink in then continued. "Obviously her mother knew there was something a bit different but hoped it may go away as she got older, rather than addressing the problem. Daphne and June however were a totally different story. They mocked her, goaded her, called her names and in general made her life a misery, but not so that everyone could see. Oh No. To the outside world they were just normal kids, teasing each other, doing all the things other children did. But it was a terrible stigma. Whereas Elsie tried to ignore it, the girls were so ashamed that one of their own could be like this. As they grew up it got worse until actual hatred was born. She was an embarrassment to them and Elsie feared they would disassociate themselves with her completely."

He paused for a moment letting this change of direction sink in but the rest knew that this was not going to be pretty and were almost ahead of him.

"How did the rest of the villagers take it?" Sunset asked.

"Who knows how they felt in general?" He replied and left it there for the moment then continued.

"Let's accept that pretty well the whole of her life was made unbearable by this sadistic pair whereas they could have got her the right kind of help, but that would have been admitting she was something different and that would never do."

Although this needed explaining, they all were anxious to get to the serious business which should throw some light on everything.

"Let me move on to when June had her spells of delving into the unknown and dabbled in, well things she didn't understand."

"Didn't stick at it, did she?" Marmaduke checked. "Not for long periods I mean."

"Quite right. It was something to fall back on when she got bored so in some ways it was nothing serious but these meddlers can open doors as we very well know."

There was a general agreement as this was something they came upon all too frequently.

"Let us move to when the travelling evangelists, or whatever they called themselves visited the area. As far as I can make out she went along to one of their gatherings and got friendly with a couple of the women who were about her age or a bit younger. Now this pair were hardly the 'holier than thou' sort, in fact they had recently had enough of this lifestyle and were looking for a way out, in fact they had suggested to their leader that they may leave the group shortly. It came as no surprise and one or two of the older members were rather relieved for this pair didn't always promote the right image."

"So these three formed a sort of friendship." Bracket said.

"Exactly. And June thought this was great at first. They were staying at the nearby market town and had suggested moving in with her eventually but that wasn't in her plan. However she kept them in tow for now."

Again he paused as if not wanting to go on but knew they were picking up on his findings and it all had to come out.

"It has to be said that these two were far from the kindest souls and the chance to have a bit of fun with someone less fortunate, or with problems gave them a thrill, so when June asked if they would like to assist with 'Pip' as her sister was known, they jumped at it."

"Help?" Bracket was trying to get it absolutely right.

"Strange you should use that word." Hashtag went on. "The plan was to tell the sister that they knew someone with a similar problem and had found help. This person would be willing to meet her but didn't want other people to know about it so it couldn't be in a public place."

"She must have wondered why, after all her life, June wanted to offer assistance." Bonnet thought.

"Quite. But when someone is that desperate, maybe it seemed a life line." Ampersand added.

The attention was back on Hashtag to continue.

"June and Daphne, oh yes she was in on it now, concocted the story that they had to go to the top road and this person would meet them, then Pip could either sit in the car and talk privately, or they could all go somewhere where they wouldn't be recognised."

"I'd have been very suspicious." Bracket said.

They all agreed but were anxious to get on with it.

"So June takes Pip and meets the two who say the person should be along any moment. Must just add that there is a small lane near the copse where they all parked and was out of sight of the road, so they would draw no attention if the odd car happened to be passing. But when a car does arrive it is Daphne plus a very unwilling Ken who was driving."

"How many more in this party?" Bonnet was adding it up.

Hashtag knew he had come to the unpleasant bit.

"The evangelist women were taunting Pip, calling her names pushing her in the semi dark, there was a bit of a moon that kept popping out from the clouds, until Daphne ordered them to hold her down. Ken had been to the boot of the car and handed something to his wife. As Pip fell to the ground, the cricket bat came down on her head many times until she no longer moved."

The Paws were piecing it all together now but Hashtag had to finish.

"As you can imagine there was silence for a moment then June ordered them to start digging in the middle of the trees. The two women suddenly panicked at the reality of what had happened and tried to escape but the sisters couldn't allow that, and while June hit one round her head with the bat, the other was killed with the spade which Daphne had grabbed off Ken."

"So they had planned to kill her and bury her with the help of these two strangers." Sunset summed up.

Bracket agreed but added "But did they plan on murdering them as well?"

"It was possible," Hashtag answered, "can't imagine having them witness that and then letting them leave can you?"

"So who buried them?" Bonnet asked.

"It would take some doing although it was quite a shallow grave." Hashtag said. "But this was one thing that had been puzzling me. Remember the smell?"

Ampersand jumped in. "The embalming fluid, you said it was very faint."

"That's right. Well at that time Ken was working for a local undertaker as well as doubling up as a grave digger at the local church."

"Ah so he would be used to it and carry some of the smell on his clothes." Marmaduke was amazed that such a small trace could have been detected.

Sunset was wondering something.

"I can't understand why Ken got involved. Surely he would stand up to his wife on something like killing her sister."

"Maybe she had something on him." One of them suggested.

To sum up at this point Marmaduke said "So all three were thrown into the grave but what was it that made you think there was something different about these women to the others?"

He knew the answer but wanted confirmation.

"Clothing." Hashtag said but I think you'd worked that out. "In this grave the two singers were dressed in feminine attire but the sister was in jeans, flat shoes etc. There had to be a reason."

They were all quiet for a moment. In their work they came across many situations but sometimes the sheer callousness of people against those that they should be helping angered them. This poor lady had only known a life of misery from her own flesh and blood, with no understanding or compassion. She was an embarrassment to them and their warped minds made them remove her. Ken was to blame for not standing up to them but as people in that situation know it is often easier said than done.

Having covered what happened twelve years ago, the question now arose as to the next move. The main task was to bring the crime to the attention of those who could deal with it in the physical world, in a way it could be proved. They could certainly expose the grave site without delay and then it would have to be up to the police to take over. But that would not affect the spiritual side, that would not be so easy to avoid for all concerned for there is no hiding place.

Sunset now broached another side to it.
"What about Elsie in all of this?"
She wondered how the daughters had explained the sudden disappearance to the mother. It seemed they lied and said she had left a note saying that she was going away and they weren't to follow her. She wanted to start a new life. Elsie had been upset that her daughter hadn't gone to her and told her or at least written to her personally but the two made excuses for that.
"But she found out when she died." Sunset almost announced. "And that's why she was so upset, because she had been oblivious of how callous her other two were." Then corrected herself. "Are."

"I think she only knew the whole truth when she had actually passed over and that's why she was not at rest." Bonnet thought.

"Which raises another question." Ampersand said. "Just going back to explaining the disappearance. What about the two other women? Surely the people where they were staying must have questioned them not going back?"

Hashtag answered that.

"Sadly their conniving was their downfall. It seems they had decided to turn up with their belongings and tell June they had nowhere to go and beg that they stay with her just until they found somewhere else. Their bill would be paid by the group who, even though they knew the two were leaving, thought it very bad manners to up and go without so much as a goodbye, or thank you."

"But their car?" Sunset asked. "What did they do with that?"

"Hired." Hashtag then answered their next question. "That was another job Ken had dumped on him."

Sunset had worked this out. "So he probably found the hirer's details in the vehicle so he'd know where it had come from. I bet Daphne made him drive it back and dump it on their forecourt, you can do that."

Bonnet suggested "And June and Daphne would have had to follow to bring him back to pick up his own."

"What a mess." Ampersand was replaying it in her thoughts.

Marmaduke had been taking all this in but it was nothing new.

"You know what they say about the best laid plans? We've seen more complicated situations from people coming across the unexpected, and what had started as a simple job turned into a nightmare. But it will always be so."

"But having to live with that. It would drive some people out of their minds." Bracket stated.

"I think it did in this case." Sunset spoke for them all.

It was time to move to the next stage but Ampersand wanted clarification on the way Elsie seemed to split into three. Marmaduke took over now.

"Actually she didn't. Don't forget she was in a very volatile state at the time and we were concerned that she was a target for any passing evil but she was also available for any other would be contacts."

"So two joined her, rather than her appearing to be three." Bonnet thought she had it.

Hashtag cut in here.

"They were possibly female relatives of the two singers, not their mothers as they are still both in body, although that cannot be disregarded completely. They could even have been friends who are now in spirit but they were certainly out for justice and homed in on Elsie hoping this would be their route to securing it."

"Ah, so they could work as one or wander around individually looking for clues." Bracket was sure of this.

Sunset couldn't help but voice her concern.

"What Elsie must have gone through. Finding out that her offspring murdered their own sister who she had carried and now she feels she has to expose her other two because of the heinous crime and the bigotry. It is so sad."

Although the rest of The Paws were in agreement, they all knew there was no time for sentiment. There was a job to be done and they had to move now.

The three gossips' main topic of conversation was the forthcoming funeral.

"It should be in the church and have done with it." Olive was disappointed she wouldn't be doing the flowers.

"Probably trying to save a bob or two." Irene's first thought was usually money.

Pam was quick to point out that nothing was cheap about it.

"They charge you for every single thing," she insisted "and folks pay up because it looks like penny pinching if you don't."

"Oh too right." Irene was back on it. "There's some do it just for the show, you know with them black horses with their nails painted and stuff."

"What you on about? "Olive demanded. "Whose nails?"

"Horses! Don't you know nothing?"

Pam cut in "Never mind about horses. We're talking about Elsie, God rest her soul. Now, God fearing woman that she was deserves to be sent off right."

"Oh yes, she deserves that. I mean it's respect that is." Olive added.

Irene tried to get back to the matter in hand.

"But we shan't be able to go. You know where that cremation place is don't you? Right out on the ring road, and I can't shut the shop for that long."

"I'd like to have paid my respects." Olive tried to look as though she meant it.

"See what's going off more like." Pam added for which she received a rather withering look.

As there was little more to talk about at the moment they agreed to meet up if anyone heard anything juicy, little guessing what was about to be unearthed on their doorstep.

Although Mary was looking forward to her marriage, she didn't want to be pushed into it without making sure everything was going to be perfect. This was something she hadn't thought could happen and she was going to make the most of every detail and although it was reassuring that Simon wanted to make her his wife as soon as he could, she stuck to her guns and said it mustn't be a rushed job. Little did she know that her guardians were steering her with caution so that she didn't take the biggest step of her life without consideration of what her new role would demand. Being a vicar's wife was an important job and she wanted to prepare herself for this step. His opinion was that he would help her all the way, but she insisted it be done properly and she wanted him to be proud of her knowing she had accomplished it by her own determination.

Planning was the most important part of The Paws' operation now for if it wasn't executed with precision, all the hard work would be for nothing and it could be years before the crimes could be exposed by which time the murderers would have died.

It was Wednesday, the day before the funeral. The question now was whether to go ahead or leave it until after Elsie had been committed, but even if police could be guided to the graves, it still had to be proved who had killed the women. With modern forensics it wouldn't take long to identify the three victims and the remaining sisters, if they had the gall could plead ignorance saying their sister had said she was going away. Of course they never expected her to be found.

After much deliberation it was decided that one day wouldn't make much difference and they wanted the women to be free from any diversion when the discovery was made so that they could monitor their every move.

Even if Elsie's earthly remains were disposed of, there was no way that she would be anywhere else for a while. She would be both at the grave where Pip would be discovered, and watching her two faced children pretending to grieve in front of their own sprogs. Her guardians were in constant attendance, not only to support her but ward off any unwelcome visitors that this sort of event always attracts. She had been through enough without any unnecessary attention.

Although Simon was not conducting the service he decided to go along to show his respects which surprised Mary as he had made no mention of it and it was against the family's wishes.

"You didn't say." She had queried.

"No but I thought I ought, after all it's not Elsie's fault she's not being laid to rest in the churchyard."

"I will only be there for the service, if you can call it that." He seemed to be making an apology but she thought that this was something she would have to get used to once they were married.

Daphne seemed to be getting more and more het up as the day came to an end whereas June was taking it in her stride. It was as though she felt she was now in charge and was riding on a cloud, knowing the dishonest pair would get their just deserts and soon. She had ordered a small wreath with just hers and Jack's names on and that would be going to the funeral directors in the morning.

"What are we sending?" Ken had asked a few times, but Daphne had fobbed him off before.

"Why, you paying for it?" She snapped.

"It's not right, you have to send a wreath."

She huffed. "Hmm. Well, I've ordered some cut flowers then we can bring them home after."

"What? It's your own mother."

"Well, you should have thought of that when you were helping me spend the money, shouldn't you?"

He sat with his head in his hands.

"Never thought it would come to this. You said nobody would ever know. That's what you said."

She slammed her fist down on the table.

"Will you stop telling me what I said." She ordered.

"It'll come out you mark my words." He was shaking his head from side to side. "June'll see to that. We're finished. I'll never be able to hold my head up again. Lived round here all my life, I have."

"All right Mr clever dick. What do you suppose we do? Go on tell me that."

"I don't know. I don't know I tell you."

They sat in silence for a moment then Daphne got up and said "Well we're not finished yet. So let's get tomorrow out of the way and have done with it. It'll all quieten down. Just a storm in a teacup. Talking of which I'll make a brew."

"Bloody big teacup." Ken muttered under his breath.

Although the format for the discovery of the grave was in place, there were certain things that were never discussed amongst The Paws. There was an understanding known only to them but which no other entity could home in on, thus protecting the element of surprise at every stage. They let the new day dawn and take its course keeping the vibrations level so that there was no suggestion of impending disturbance.

Simon, true to his word attended the funeral, said a few words to the mourners that were there and left. Never had he experienced such a fake atmosphere for although the daughters were snivelling into their hankies there were no tears. It was almost as if it never happened and he hoped Elsie hadn't witnessed it.

"What did he want?" Daphne whispered to Ken.

"Paid his respects, that's all. Stop being dramatic."

June spent the whole proceedings slightly apart from the others with her nose in the air. She spoke only to Simon and the celebrant and left in her own car.

"Well, how do you like that?" Daphne was indignant. "I paid for her tea."

"I shouldn't worry," Ken assured her, "There's never very much and I can soon polish off hers."

"That's not the point." She was determined to have the last word.

Chapter 11

It was time for The Paws to put the next phase into operation,
 "Shall we use the vicar?" Marmaduke suggested.
 There was some consternation at that thought.
 "Bit naughty." Hashtag observed but then added "Why not? Got to have someone."
 It was late Thursday afternoon, dry and fairly mild so visibility was good which was important. The thought had been put into Simon's head to use the top road on the way home although he imagined it was his own idea. He was approaching the little group of trees when he saw a large dog standing in the middle of the road. He braked and as he slowed down the dog barked and moved into the trees, only to reappear and bark at him again. Simon was always wary when driving on a lonely road and this could be a trap, but the dog appeared agitated and seemed to be asking him to follow him.
 There was a small patch of ground at the side of the road where people often parked for a while, so he pulled over and stopped. From there he could see the dog pawing at the ground.
 Slowly Simon got out and called "What's up chap? Found a bone?" Words which he would always remember. The dog looked at him and back at the ground. Not knowing the animal, or if it may attack he moved very cautiously forward but as he approached, the dog moved back almost assuring him it was safe.
 Then the vicar saw it. It was a bone, partly sticking out of the soil. Something made him keep his distance and he went to his car, grabbed his mobile and called the police saying it may

be nothing but something was obviously buried there and he would wait for them to arrive to show them the place.

It took a while for a car to come from the nearest town but they assured him they had come straight away. Asking him to point to the spot but stay back they gingerly made their way forward until they were near the protruding bone. One officer immediately got onto his radio to call specialist help while the other asked what made Simon notice it.

"Stopped for a pee?" he joked.

"No, it was…" he stopped. "It's gone."

"What's gone sir?" The policeman looked around.

Simon explained how the dog was in the road and how he had led him to the place but he seemed to have gone.

"Could be a stray, in which case it'll get shot if the farmer finds it worrying his livestock." Was the officer's thought.

The other PC returned and said others were on the way and they were to make sure nobody entered the wood. Having got Simon's details and because of his profession they decided he could go but they would be in touch. They also told him not to speak of it to anyone at all even family. He knew that meant he couldn't even confide in Mary but in his job he was used to keeping his own council.

As he drove home he little guessed what the outcome would be and how it could affect his future happiness.

Elsie had taken little interest in her funeral, after all she had no more use for her body yet her spirit had a lot to do and there were many questions surrounding all the new information. One of the guardians had directed her to the vicar's cupboard where she had found a small ankle chain that she knew belonged to Pip. She'd bought it as a present many years before and recognised it immediately but obviously wondered why he had it. When she checked Mary's house, she was satisfied there was nothing similar there. Now she had to find out what Simon knew. She appreciated that he must hear many things in his job but if there was something here she should be aware of, she was determined to know what it was.

This had nothing to do with the other two poor souls who she learned were grieving their granddaughters although they offered any help for they wanted the whole truth to come out no matter how painful and let the perpetrators pay for eternity.

The next move was going to be difficult but The Paws had their ways. They moved Elsie and her two colleagues to a secluded place and instructed them to wait but be prepared for an emotional moment. As they settled, they were aware of other presences near them.

"Mum." Elsie recognised the voice through her spirit awareness.

"Gran."

"Nanna."

They all heard it. If they had been in body the tears would have flowed copiously but in spirit the emotion is equal if not greater and the next moments were for them to share, in private. A secure guard was placed around them so that nothing could harm them in their delicate state.

After a very testing reunion all six were told to share any memory they had, no matter how painful. They split off into pairs, the singers with their grandmothers and Pip with Elsie who felt she should apologise as it was her daughters who were the cause of all this pain. Now these six were determined and united to do all in their power to expose them.

It was not a time to hold back and Pip knew she had to be honest with her mother, not only for herself but for the sake of the innocent ones.

Elsie was anxious to know why the Simon had the ankle chain.

"I went to see him. It must have slipped off, I always wondered. He was at the All Saints parish at the time. I'd been to our vicar who said I was evil and making it all up and I would burn in hell."

"What?" Elsie was shocked.

"Well I was telling him how the girls were making my life unbearable and I was near doing myself in. It was mental torture and I didn't know where to turn."

"But you could have come to us." Elsie felt guilty.

"I tried but you passed it off. It was like if you ignored it, it would go away, but it didn't. Those things don't."

Elsie was still trying to get it straight.

"Tell me honestly what Daphne and June did. All of it." Elsie had to know now, even if it was too late.

It wasn't a pretty tale. The two soon realised she was a bit different and it started with simple jibes, then mocking, name calling and physical abuse. They even stripped her one day to see if she had anything they hadn't, as they put it. Then they used to joke with their friends until she was almost an outcast at school. Of course it didn't stop there but carried on into adulthood. They even told her she was marked by the devil and not to expect any decent person to want her or they would expose her for what she was. By this time her poor mind had become so sick she actually believed it and the thought of help didn't enter her head.

"But you went to the vicar." Elsie reminded her.

"I didn't want to, because of what the other one had said but I'd seen him once and thought he looked kind."

"And was he, to you I mean?"

"He seemed to be, but I just didn't trust anyone then. He said he could get me some help but I knew that would mean talking to strangers and I couldn't. I was going to at one point but chickened out. Couldn't do it."

Elsie gave her the biggest spiritual hug to make up for all the times she hadn't been there for her and knew it would take a long time for the guilt to go.

"I wonder why he kept your chain." Elsie was curious.

Pip answered that. "He wouldn't have known where to find me then."

There was a moments' hesitation while the mum weighed up the timing.

"When you disappeared," she couldn't bear to use the proper words "that would be about two years before he came to our parish."

"Suppose so."

"And he would know who we were eventually."

Pip wondered where this was going.

"What are you getting at?"

"So why didn't he find out and return your chain to me?"

There was a stillness in the air for some time.

Eventually Elsie said "If he found it and popped it in a safe place hoping to see you again, that's one thing. Or when you put something somewhere for now, you tend to forget it's there and it slips out of sight. But it was in plain sight in the cupboard, near the front of the little shelf as though it was there on purpose."

"Oh."

Pip was confused but didn't put too much meaning into it although it was niggling at Elsie.

The other two women had enjoyed being reunited with their grandmas and would have carried on longer but they knew that the truth was about to be unearthed, literally and when forensic got their hands on the remains the identities would be revealed.

As soon as the news got out, there would be more than one person sweating profusely.

"What did you make of the parson?" One of the police patrol asked his mate.

"Dunno. Actually, come to think of it, if I'd been in his boots I'd have been a bit more shocked."

"Hmm. More surprised than he was you might say."

His partner was thinking it a bit strange. "Wonder where the dog went, if there was one."

"I suppose it's like this job, you see all sorts and yet you never cease to be surprised. I mean he must come across deaths all the time."

"Well yeah, in hospital, in folks own beds, accidents. That kind of shit."

"But we don't know what that bone is yet. May be nothing."

"Got a feeling in my water there is. We'll have to wait and see."

The Paws were monitoring not only the site but also everyone else involved. While they waited for the ground to be excavated they wondered if this had been a copy cat crime. If someone had heard, or had knowledge of the USA and Canada events they could easily make this one look as though the same person had a hand in it but with all the facts to date it was decided it was pure coincidence from the physical angle. Whether or not a spiritual connection was uncovered in later years would remain to be seen. One could never completely close the file.

"Do you know what you remind me of?" Bracket asked Hashtag.

"I dread to think." Was the abrupt reply but he knew he would find out shortly.

"Well it's like a computer. You see, people think they have hidden evidence, that is they have pressed the delete key. But it is still stored on the hard drive if you know how to retrieve it. Well you do. Retrieve it I mean."

"Is that it?"

"Well yes." Bracket was disappointed as he thought he'd paid the cat a compliment.

The rest were amused but had to admit he had a point, it was very much like that. Somewhere, and somehow everything was there to be found, if you knew how to do it.

Simon walked slowly into the vicarage. His gut feeling, or spiritual guidance whatever he called it was making him feel very uneasy. For some reason he went to his bedroom, opened the cupboard and took out the chain holding it in his hands as if for inspiration. He sat on the edge of the bed and a feeling of extreme despair swept over him and he remembered the woman's face. Suddenly he felt a blow to the back of his head which knocked him forward. Thinking he had been attacked he turned to face whoever was there, but he was alone. He got up and sat back on the bed with the tremendous guilt that he had let the owner of this chain down. Instinctively he knew she was in the wood and he had been led to find her but this was something he couldn't share with anyone. But that was not all that was lying heavy on his heart.

It didn't take long for word to get around that something had happened on the top road near the villages. Part of the field was cordoned off and there were forensic vehicles along with police cars, so something serious must have happened.

By Friday morning every village and neighbouring town knew about it and when the press started arriving the gossips went into overdrive. The speculation knew no bounds but already there were some very worried people who knew the truth.

Before Olive went to work she was round at the shop where Irene and Pam were already trying to work it out. They came up with all sorts of suggestions and were eager to put their point forward just in case they were right when it all was announced and they could get some mileage for being the one to guess correctly, saying of course they knew all along.

Mary was getting ready for work and noticed the time. Strange that Simon hadn't rung her already. It had become a little personal ritual that they rang each other and said goodnight just before getting into bed and good morning as soon as they were awake. Sometimes he had been up all night if someone was near death so she had learned to take it in her stride. Not wanting to wake him if this was the case, she left at her usual time.

As soon as she walked into work all the staff were upon her.

"What can you tell us? What happened? Have you seen it?"

"Now just a minute." She held up her hand. "I don't know what you're talking about."

There was a barrage of questions so one of the staff shouted for them to quieten down and let one person speak.

"On the top road near your village, it's heaving with police and stuff."

Her heart sank. Was that why Simon hadn't phoned?

"Please, I know nothing. I must make a phone call."

She hurried from the office almost in tears and used her mobile. Eventually he answered but she could tell there was something wrong.

"Simon, Simon, what is it?"

"I can't talk now. We will speak when you get home."

She was frantic. "How am I supposed to work all day?"

"Look dearest, it's church business, I can't say any more than that. You know my position. Please don't worry I am alright."

"Promise." She wasn't satisfied but had no option but to accept what he said, but as she ended the call she had the feeling he wasn't alone so maybe that's why he couldn't say anything just then. That must be it.

Ken had gone to work as normal and as he passed the cordoned off area he felt physically sick. They must have found the bodies, or what was left of them. It couldn't be anything else but if he kept his head down and his wife kept her mouth shut, they shouldn't be involved. However it preyed on his mind until he had to stop the car and empty his breakfast in a ditch. He now felt ghastly and wondered how he would cope, but if he didn't go to work it could look suspicious and he must keep a face on things. He was grateful he no longer worked for the undertaker as that would have been traumatic. He worried if Daphne would keep her cool and couldn't wait to get home so he could keep an eye on her. And what about June, but she wasn't likely to go admitting anything.

By lunchtime there was a report on the radio and also on the local television channel.

The Paws weren't sure whether to be surprised by June's reaction, for as the news filtered through it seemed to sweep over her as though it had nothing to do with her whatsoever. But in her mind it hadn't. As the years had gone on, she had conditioned herself to really believe she was innocent and her sister and brother in law were the sole villains. They had proved themselves to be underhand and deceitful the way they stole their mother's money, her money she considered it to be now, so let them take the rap for everything. That would be justice done. She went about with a half smile on her face feeling very pleased with the way things had worked out.

"Don't come crying to me when you are exposed for what you are." She crowed. "You will deserve everything you get and I hope you rot in jail."

Most people would be left open mouthed at her attitude, but The Paws had seen it many times and sad as it may be, there would always be people like that, who never took the blame. It was always someone else.

It was reaching the stage where the physical authorities would gather their evidence and take over to administer their justice as far as those in body were concerned. But the implementation of spiritual justice is a different matter. On earth, a criminal pays the fine or serves the time and often that is the end of it but it is different in other realms. The churches teach that God is all loving, all forgiving and if you repent, your sins will be forgiven. But this is not just a way out. 'Oh dear I'm sorry, slap my wrist. That's alright then, I can go and do it again.' That is not how it works in spiritual justice.

In spirit you have to learn that you must permanently change your ways, your thoughts, and certainly the way you interact with others. You cannot proceed to higher levels until you have achieved this and would for eternity exist either in an earth bound state, or on the lowest of spiritual planes. Many have been told it is no good saying 'well I'm being good so far, so that's ok'. It is not. Although it may appear harsh to the untrained, or those with different beliefs, it will become very apparent when the time comes for each soul to go through transition. It is not an easy ride.

So while the likes of June, Daphne and Ken would await their eventual earthly sentences, preparation would already be in place to try and make them into worthy spirits, to ensure they appreciated the way they had treated a fellow soul, to feel true remorse for the heinous crimes and learn penitence. That could take many earth years to achieve, but there would be no guarantee.

The Paws' job was to monitor the earthly happenings and try and intervene to prevent the horror and masochistic torture that thrives in certain people thus preparing them for specialised counselling and a chance of future peace. But they would be the first to admit that none of them are soft when it comes to getting results, in fact some would say that on occasions they were downright callous but sometimes, with some subjects it was necessary.

Simon was on his knees his hands together in prayer. Being a vicar had its advantages, there were some very happy occasions to share with people but at times like this the burden weighed heavily on him and he prayed for the strength he needed to cope with the situation. For all the training he'd received, it still didn't prepare him for how he would feel when faced with such a task. He now asked for forgiveness and knew he had acted as he should but it didn't take the guilt away.

A few years ago, Ken had come to see him privately and being assured that whatever he divulged to a vicar could not be reported, he confessed to all that had gone on that terrible night. It had nearly driven him out of his mind and he had to tell someone. His wife was no consolation, threatening that he would take the entire blame if he opened his mouth, after all she couldn't possibly have had the strength to kill somebody. Simon did his best to try and get him to talk to the police with him present for support but there was no way he would even consider it and began to regret his visit. There was no option but to keep the news to himself and never give any clue as to his knowledge of it. Therefore when he saw the dog leading him to the trees, although he didn't know the location, as soon as he saw the bone he guessed that this must be it. He prayed it wasn't and was just an animal that had been run over, but his gut feeling told him that was not the case.

Now he was pretty certain he had his answer but what could he do? He could hardly go round to Ken and say 'Oh its ok, they've found her.' It was torment waiting, but he had to be strong.

He was also upset by the fact that sisters, or even anybody could do such a thing to another living being. What was in their make up that allowed it? He stayed in prayer for some time, not knowing how he was going to face the world with this weight round his shoulders. Although he had carried it in secret for a time, it would be more difficult when the facts came to light. How would Mary feel about him then? He even questioned his vocation and wondered if he had failed.

Elsie had formed quite a bond with the grandmothers who held no grudge against her and even felt her pain and guilt. But these three were determined to make sure that the two women and Ken got their punishment even if they had to enlist good powers to help them. But they need not have worried for the truth would be discovered and then there would be a lot of explaining to do. They may have thought they had been clever in the past, but they would not be up to the intense questioning and it was more a case of who would crack first.

"My money's on Ken." Bracket announced but before anyone else could show their preference, Marmaduke reminded them of the gravity of the situation.

"Even when their earthly term of punishment is over, it's only the beginning."

Often when a case was drawing to a close, it was tempting to hang around and watch the outcome, but with the workload always waiting The Paws didn't enjoy such a luxury.

"Can I still pop back and see if I was right?" Bracket couldn't resist asking but the 'tale wave' gave him his answer.

Marmaduke did raise one ongoing factor.

"The preacher man has kept a low profile in this life and I don't think he cottoned on to us although we did pick up a few useful observations."

"I can't understand why he isn't undergoing cleansing." Sunset said.

They were referring to the one who had raped the three women in Niagara and the three in Pennsylvania. After his untimely passing, he had made a quick return to earth and would need careful observation but caution must be observed as he could change his tactics in this life.

"Well he won't be idle." Bracket thought.

"Let's not forget he isn't that high up so he's not that powerful." Ampersand reminded them.

Marmaduke was looking ahead "It's who he could team up with. He could end up being some evil thing's toy, to do their bidding, but thinking it was his own doing. They con them like that as we well know."

"Watch and wait then." Bonnet stated then asked. "Who's going to take him on board?"

"We all are." Marmaduke decided. "It's not him, he's not shrewd enough, as we agree it's who is going to use him. Some higher power wouldn't know it was us but would soon pick up it was a high force they were dealing with. Therefore we slip in and out at varying intervals."

"He will do something. He can't help it." Sunset said regretfully. "And it's what he could easily become."

And so the former preacher man was on the list unbeknown to June who had named him Wizard. But he would shortly be finding a new home.

It was also time to recall the other two members of The Paws who had been riding tandem through this operation in order to mingle and observe without being recognised but still operating from a distance. They weren't ones for fancy names and were laughingly referred to as Dot and Com. Dot had been a passenger with Mary and Com had been riding with Irene. These were useful tactics as from the most unlikely source a very important snippet could be retrieved that could prove to be the most important factor in the outcome.

Chapter 12

Apart from Marmaduke the beautiful long haired ginger, often referred to as 'the golden cat', none of the others have been described but for those who wish to know, on this occasion they chose to be :-

A short haired pure white
A long haired smoky grey
A domestic black and white
A Siamese
A Manx
A silver grey tabby
and of course
A brown tabby

But which one was which? We leave that for you to decide.

The Paws now rose up away from the earth and started to merge, their images forming a beautiful mix of colours until only the eyes identified them. Gradually they faded away until there was nothing to be seen because The Paws did not exist. As cats they did not exist. They were simply an almighty power of good, stronger than anything known to any level. As a group they would always be a myth, but the work they did and what they achieved would be felt in some way by many, both on earth and in spirit. They were the ultimate in divine perfection and spiritual justice.

- - - - - - - - - - - -

If you ever feel at the end, and you have sunk into a dark pit, and if something you don't understand pulls you out and helps you back onto your feet, you have been blessed with the help of a very special power, call it whatever name you like.

About the Author

Tabbie Browne grew up in the Cotswolds in central England which is where she gets the inspiration for her novels. Her father had very strong spiritual beliefs and she feels he guides her but always with a warning to stay in control of your own mind.

Her earliest recollection of writing was at primary school and it has seemed to play a part at significant times during her life. She thinks it is only when we are forced to take step back and unclutter our minds for a while we realise our potential. This point was proved when she slipped a disc, and being very immobile had to write in pencil as the ink would not flow upwards! At this time she wrote many comical poems which, when able again, performed to many audiences. Comedy is very difficult but you know if you are a success with a live audience.

In 1991 as a collector of novelty salt and pepper shakers, she realised there was no book in the UK devoted entirely to the subject. So she wrote one. Which meant she achieved the fact that it was the first of its kind in the country and it sold well to like collectors not only in the UK but in the USA.

Another large upheaval came when she was diagnosed with breast cancer, and due to the extreme energy draining, found it difficult to work for an employer. So she took a freelance journalist course and was pleased to have articles accepted, her main joy being the piece about her father and his life in the village. Again the inspiration area.

But the novels were eating away inside and drawing on her experience at stamp and coin fairs she wrote *'A Fair Collection'* which she serialised in the magazine 'Squirrels' for people who hoard things.

When she wrote *'White Noise Is Heavenly Blue'* and its sequel *'The Spiral'* she sat at the keyboard and the titles just came to her, as did the content of the books. There is no way she could write the plot first as she never knew what was coming next, almost as if somebody was dictating, and for that reason she could never change anything.

Loves:
Animals,
Also performing in live theatre and working as a tv supporting artiste.

Hates:
Bad manners,
Insincere people.